Crossroads & Connections

La'Shayla Godfrey

www.theinkwellpublishingcompany.com

ISBN: 979-8-89502-004-3 (hardback) | 979-8-89502-005-0 (paperback) | 979-8-89502-006-7 (ebook)

Publication Data
Subjects: Coming of Age; Romance; New Experience
Keyword: Loving the small moments of college life
Short Description: A must-read for anyone who believes that connection and understanding can triumph over life's challenges.

This is a work of fiction inspired by the author's imagination and experiences. While elements of the story may draw from reality, any resemblance to actual persons, organizations, or events—beyond those intentionally referenced—is entirely coincidental.

Printed in the United States of America
1st Printing
Editor: Demetri D. Long
Cover Designer & Illustrator: La'Shayla Godfrey
Formator: Demetri D. Long

Chapter 1
Goodbye, Comfort Zone

Nia tightened her grip on the suitcase handle as they stood in front of the towering brick dorm building. The buzz of students and parents bustling around them was almost too much to take in—cars double-parked, friends reuniting, and the low hum of nervous conversations filling the air. It was supposed to be exciting, but all Nia felt was the sinking weight of uncertainty.

They'd spent the past eighteen years in the same quiet town where everyone knew their name and every street felt like a familiar shortcut. Now, standing in the middle of this sea of strangers, Nia wasn't sure if she was ready for what came next.

"Do you need help with that?" Her mom's voice cut through the noise, soft but firm. She was holding one end of a box labeled *'Winter Clothes - Don't Open Until October'* with duct tape that looked like it had already been peeled and re-stuck several times.

"No, I've got it," Nia said quickly, adjusting her grip. Her dad stood nearby, fidgeting with the car keys like he was trying to keep busy. They hadn't said much on the drive, and now it seemed like the weight of unspoken words was hanging in the air between them.

The three of them made their way inside the dorm, the cool blast of air conditioning a welcome relief from the late-summer heat. The hallway smelled like fresh paint and faintly of someone's burnt popcorn. Nia glanced at the room numbers as they passed, finally stopping in front of *804*.

"Here we are," her dad said, his voice bright but forced. He pushed the door open, revealing a small but clean room with two twin beds, two desks, and a single window that barely let in any light. One side of the room was already claimed, with a pile of books and a bright orange comforter draped across the bed.

"This is nice," her mom said, setting down the box and looking around. Nia couldn't tell if she was being genuine or just trying to fill the silence.

She dropped her suitcase near the empty bed and took a deep breath. It wasn't home, but it wasn't terrible either.

A voice startled them from the doorway. "You must be Nia."

Nia turned to see a short, confident-looking girl standing casually in front of the door. She had brown and black braids that were neat and in two messy buns and wore a denim jacket despite the heat outside.

"Yeah, that's me," Nia replied, hesitantly offering a small smile.

"I'm Zahara."

"The best roommate you will ever have!" Zahara stepped inside and gave me a high five before tossing a duffel bag onto her bed, "Hope you don't snore!"

Nia blinked, unsure how to respond. "Uh, I don't think so?"

"Good enough for me," Zahara said, flopping onto her bed like she'd already conquered the room.

Nia's mom gave a polite smile, clearly trying to assess whether Zahara was someone her child should be living with. "It's nice to meet you, Zahara."

Zahara waved casually. "You too. Don't worry, I'll take good care of your kid."

Nia felt a bit embarrassed. "I'm not a kid," she mumbled under her breath.

Zahara grinned as she heard, but thankfully didn't push it.

After a few minutes of awkward small talk and unpacking, Nia's parents said their goodbyes. Her mom pulled them into a tight hug. "You're going to do great," she said, though her voice wavered slightly.

Her dad patted her shoulder and gave a gruff, "Call us if you need anything."

And just like that, they were gone.

Nia stood in the middle of the room, the silence pressing in now that the bustle of moving in was over. Zahara was already rifling through a box, pulling out posters and random knickknacks to decorate her side of the room.

"So, where are you from?" Zahara asked, breaking the silence.

"Uh, MapleGrove. It's a small town, about two hours from here," Nia said, sitting on her bed and trying not to feel awkward.

Zahara raised an eyebrow. "Small town, huh? Bet this is a big change for you."

"You could say that."

Zahara nodded like she understood, but there was a glimmer of amusement in their eyes. "Don't worry. You'll adjust. The first week is always weird."

Before Nia could respond, Zahara's phone buzzed. She glanced at it and sighed. "I've gotta go meet some people downstairs. You okay here?"

"Yeah, I'm fine," Nia said, though she wasn't sure it was true.

"Cool. Catch you later," Zahara said, grabbing her keys and heading out the door.

The room felt strangely empty after Zahara left. Nia stared at the half-unpacked suitcase, suddenly unsure where to start. She pulled out a few shirts and hung them in the closet, but the task felt meaningless.

To distract herself, she grabbed her phone and scrolled through messages. A few friends from high school had sent quick "Good luck!" texts, but there wasn't much else. She opened her group chat from back home, only to find that the conversation had already shifted to local gossip that Nia no longer had any connection to.

It was a strange feeling—being in a new place but still clinging to pieces of the old one.

After a while, Nia wandered over to the window and looked

out. The view wasn't much—just a patch of grass and a parking lot—but she could see people walking by, laughing and talking like they'd already known each other for years.

Nia sighed. Maybe Zahara was right. The first week would be weird. But the weight of everything—leaving home, meeting new people, figuring out who they wanted to be—felt heavier than Nia expected.

She sank onto the bed and pulled out a journal she'd brought from home. Flipping to a blank page, they wrote three words at the top: *Who am I?*

It was a question they'd never really thought about before. Back in MapleGrove, she was just Nia—quiet, reliable, and perfectly average. But here, in this strange, new place, it felt like the answer could be anything.

The thought was both terrifying and exciting.

Nia set the journal aside and laid back on the bed, staring at the ceiling. Maybe tomorrow would feel easier. Maybe she'd figure it out, one piece at a time.

For now, though, all she could do was wait and hope that the weight of change wasn't too much to carry.

Nia woke up the next morning to the sound of laughter echoing from the hallway. For a moment, she forgot where she was. The ceiling above wasn't the familiar one from her bedroom in Maplegrove. This one was a dull beige with a single crack running through it. It was a small detail, but it cemented the realization: she wasn't home anymore.

Across the room, Zahara was sprawled out on her bed, one arm draped dramatically over her face. Nia sat up slowly, trying not to disturb the relative quiet. Her phone buzzed on the desk, and she grabbed it, grateful for the distraction.

Mom: Let us know how your first night went. Love you.

Nia hesitated, her thumbs hovering over the keyboard.

Finally, she typed: *It was fine. Miss you guys too.*

The truth was more complicated. The room had felt too big and too small all at once like it didn't quite belong to her yet.

And despite Zahara's lighthearted jokes the day before, Nia couldn't shake the feeling that they were on completely different wavelengths. Zahara had this effortless confidence that made the world seem easy to navigate. Nia, on the other hand, felt like she was wandering in the dark without a map.

"Morning," Zahara mumbled, her voice muffled by the pillow.

"Morning," Nia replied, trying to sound more awake than they felt.

Zahara rolled over and stretched. "First day of freedom. What's the plan?"

Nia blinked. "Uh, I thought classes didn't start until tomorrow?"

"Exactly," Zahara said, sitting up with a grin. "Which means today's the perfect day to explore. You can't stay cooped up in here like a hermit."

"I wasn't planning to—"

Zahara raised an eyebrow. "Were you, though?"

Nia felt a bit conflicted. She had briefly considered spending the day organizing her desk and maybe taking a walk around campus, but Zahara's teasing made them rethink it.

"Come on," Zahara said, grabbing a denim jacket from the back of her chair. "There's a coffee shop just off campus I've been dying to check out. It'll be fun."

Nia hesitated. Exploring sounded nice, but the idea of being surrounded by strangers in an unfamiliar place made her chest tighten.

"Don't overthink it," Zahara added, like she could read Nia's mind. "It's just coffee. Worst case, you hate it, and we come back here. No big deal."

Nia sighed. "Okay, fine. Let me get dressed." The coffee shop, a cozy place called *Bean & Leaf,* was bustling with students when they arrived. Zahara led the way, weaving through the crowd with the kind of ease Nia could only envy.

"This place is perfect," Zahara said, her eyes lighting up as she scanned the chalkboard menu. "What's your go-to coffee order?"

"Uh, I don't really drink coffee," Nia admitted, feeling out of place.

Zahara gave her a look of mock horror. "No coffee? How do you survive?"

"I usually just stick to tea," Nia said with a shrug.

"Tea it is, then," Zahara declared, stepping up to the counter.

A few minutes later, they found a small table by the window. Zahara sipped her iced latte with the kind of satisfaction that made Nia wonder if she was missing out on some universal experience.

"So," Zahara began, leaning forward, "what's your story, Nia from Maplegrove?"

Nia blinked. "My story?"

"Yeah. Everyone's got one. A small-town kid like you probably has some juicy secrets," Zahara teased.

Nia couldn't help but laugh, even though she felt a twinge of defensiveness. "Maplegrove isn't that exciting. It's just... quiet. Everyone knows everyone, and nothing really changes."

Zahara nodded thoughtfully. "Sounds nice. Kind of the opposite of where I grew up."

Nia tilted their head. "Where's that?"

"Chicago," Zahara said with a grin. "It's loud, chaotic, and impossible to be invisible, which I guess is a good thing sometimes."

Nia tried to picture Zahara in a big city like Chicago and realized it wasn't hard to imagine. Zahara seemed like she belonged anywhere like she could adapt to any situation without breaking a sweat.

"What made you pick this school?" Nia asked.

Zahara hesitated for a moment, her grin faltering. "It's complicated," she said finally. "But let's just say I needed a change."

The answer felt deliberately vague, but Nia decided not to press. Everyone had their reasons, and she wasn't sure Zahara was ready to share hers just yet. By the time they left the coffee shop, Nia felt a little lighter. Zahara's easygoing nature made it hard to stay in her own head for too long.

As they walked back to campus, Zahara nudged Nia with her elbow. "So, are you glad you didn't hide in the dorm all day?"

Nia smiled. "Yeah, I guess so."

"See? I told you," Zahara said with a wink. "Stick with me, and you'll survive this place."

Nia wasn't sure about a lot of things, but she was starting to think Zahara might be right about that. That evening, Nia sat at her desk, staring at the journal she'd brought from home. The question she'd written the night before— *Who am I?*—still hung in the air, unanswered.

She picked up a pen and started writing again, the words flowing more easily this time:

Today, I stepped outside my comfort zone. It wasn't as scary as I thought it would be.

She paused, tapping the pen against the page.

Maybe Zahara's right. Maybe change isn't always a bad thing.

The sound of the door opening pulled Nia from her thoughts. Zahara walked in, holding a box of pizza and a mischievous grin.

"Dinner," she announced, setting the box on the desk. "Figured you could use a break from whatever deep thoughts you're having over there."

Nia laughed. "Thanks."

She sat down and opened the box, the smell of melted cheese and garlic filling the room.

"You know," Zahara said between bites, "college is all about figuring out who you are. But no one ever said you have to do it alone."

Nia glanced at Zahara, surprised by the sudden seriousness in their tone.

"Thanks," Nia said quietly.

Zahara grinned again, the moment of seriousness passing. "Don't get used to it. I'm not always this wise."

Nia couldn't help but laugh. For the first time since arriving on campus, they felt like maybe—just maybe—they were exactly where they were supposed to be.

Nia stood in front of her mirror, adjusting the hem of her favorite sweatshirt. The faded green fabric was soft and familiar, a small comfort in a day already brimming with newness. She tried to focus on that as she slid her sneakers on, but her stomach churned with a mix of excitement and dread.

Zahara, leaning against the doorframe, gave her a look of exaggerated impatience. "You ready yet, Maplegrove? We don't have all day."

Nia rolled her eyes but couldn't stop the small smile tugging at her lips. "I'm ready. Where are we even going?"

"You'll see," Zahara said with a wink, grabbing her keys.

As they stepped out into the bright afternoon sun, Nia felt the hum of activity on campus like a tangible force. Groups of students lounged on the grassy quad, music, and laughter spilling out of open windows. She tried not to shrink under the weight of it all, but she couldn't help feeling like an outsider.

Zahara, on the other hand, moved through the crowd with the kind of confidence that drew people in. Her long strides carried her effortlessly, and she seemed to know exactly where she was going.

"Have you been here before?" Nia asked, struggling to keep up.

"Nope," Zahara said with a grin. "But I've got a good sense of direction. It's a gift."

Nia wasn't sure if she believed that, but she followed anyway.

They ended up at a small park just off campus, a quiet spot with shaded benches and a fountain that sparkled in the sunlight. Zahara flopped onto a bench and motioned for Nia to join her.

"So," Zahara began, leaning back and stretching her arms behind her head. "What's your game plan for this whole college thing?"

Nia frowned. "Game plan?"

"Yeah. Everyone's got one, even if they don't admit it.

Some people are here to reinvent themselves. Others just want to survive and get their degree. Me? I'm here to see what sticks."

Nia laughed softly. "That sounds very... flexible."

"Exactly," Zahara said, grinning. "What about you?"

Nia hesitated, picking at the edge of her sleeve. "I don't know. I guess I'm just trying to figure things out."

Zahara tilted her head, studying Nia with a curious expression. "Fair enough. But don't wait too long, or this place will figure you out before you get the chance to decide for yourself."

The words lingered in Nia's mind as they walked back to the dorm later. She wasn't sure what Zahara meant, but she suspected it was the kind of advice she'd only understand much later—once it was too late to do anything about it.

That evening, Zahara convinced Nia to join her at the campus welcome event. It was held in the student union, which had been transformed into a chaotic swirl of lights, music, and people. Nia hesitated at the entrance, overwhelmed by the sheer energy of the room.

"Don't overthink it," Zahara said, tugging her inside.

Easier said than done, Nia thought. She stuck close to Zahara as they wove through the crowd, stopping occasionally to chat with people Zahara seemed to know already.

"How do you do that?" Nia asked after Zahara greeted her fifth new acquaintance in little to no minutes.

"Do what?"

"Talk to people like it's the easiest thing in the world."

Zahara shrugged, her expression softening. "You just pretend it is. Most people are too worried about how they look to notice if you're nervous."

Nia wasn't sure she believed that, but she nodded anyway.

As the night went on, Nia found herself relaxing just a little. She even managed to join in on a few conversations, though she mostly listened. By the time they left, she felt a strange mixture of exhaustion and accomplishment.

Back in their dorm room, Zahara flopped onto her bed with a satisfied sigh. "Not bad for a first night, huh?"

Nia sat on her own bed, kicking off her shoes. "It wasn't terrible."

"That's the spirit," Zahara said with a laugh.

Nia spent the morning unpacking the last of her things, arranging books on her desk, and pinning a photo of her family to the corkboard above it. The photo was from her high school graduation, her parents beaming with pride as they stood beside her. She stared at it for a moment, a pang of homesickness tightening her chest.

Her phone buzzed on the desk, pulling her from her thoughts.

Zahara: Get dressed. We're going on an adventure.

Nia smiled despite herself.

Their "adventure" turned out to be a walk to the edge of campus, where Zahara had heard rumors of a hidden garden behind the science building. They found it tucked away between two hedges, a small oasis of flowers and benches that seemed untouched by the bustle of campus life.

"This is amazing," Nia said, her voice hushed as if speaking too loudly would disturb the peace.

Zahara grinned, clearly pleased with herself. "Told you I had a good sense of direction."

They sat on one of the benches, the scent of flowers heavy in the air.

"So, tell me more about Maplegrove," Zahara said, leaning back and closing her eyes.

Nia hesitated. "There's not much to tell. It's small. Quiet. Everyone knows everyone."

Zahara opened one eye, ignoring the repetition in their dialogue. "Sounds cozy."

"It is," Nia admitted. "But it's also... predictable. Like, you know exactly what your life is going to look like before it even happens."

"Is that why you left?" Zahara asked.

Nia nodded. "Yeah. I guess I wanted something different. I just didn't realize how hard 'different' was going to be."

Zahara was quiet for a moment, her expression thoughtful.

"Hard doesn't mean bad, though. Sometimes it just means you're doing something that matters."

The words settled over Nia like a warm blanket. She didn't say anything, but she felt a small spark of hope flicker to life in her chest.

That night, as Nia lay in bed staring at the ceiling, she thought about Zahara's words. Maybe she was right. Maybe hard didn't mean bad.

She reached for her journal and opened it to the page she'd started the day before. Picking up her pen, she wrote:

Day 2: I think I'm starting to get it. Maybe this is what change feels like—not knowing where you're going, but deciding to keep walking anyway.

With that, she closed the journal and turned off the light, letting herself drift to sleep.

The sound of Nia's alarm jolted her awake the next morning. For a moment, she couldn't remember where she was. Then it hit her—college, the dorm, a new life. She groaned and rolled over, shutting off the alarm with a swipe before sitting up and rubbing the sleep from her eyes.

Zahara was still asleep, her face buried in her pillow and her hair a chaotic halo around her head. Nia stifled a laugh, quietly getting ready for the day.

Today was the first day of classes. Nia's schedule wasn't packed, but the thought of navigating unfamiliar hallways and meeting professors made her stomach twist. She grabbed her bag and slipped out of the room, letting the door click shut softly behind her.

The campus buzzed with activity. Students rushed between buildings, clutching notebooks and coffee cups, while others lingered in groups, chatting and laughing. Nia clutched her schedule like a lifeline, double-checking it every few minutes to make sure she was heading in the right direction.

Her first class was Intro to Psychology, held in a large lecture hall that felt more like a movie theater than a classroom. Nia found a seat near the middle, hoping it was inconspicuous enough to avoid drawing attention.

As the room filled, a girl with short curly hair and glasses sat down beside her. She smiled warmly. "Hey, I'm Taylor. Mind if I sit here?"

Nia shook her head, returning the smile. "Not at all. I'm Nia."

"First-year?" Taylor asked, pulling out a laptop.

"Tell me about it. I've already gotten lost twice."

By the time the professor started the lecture, Nia felt a little less alone. Taylor's easy friendliness reminded her that she wasn't the only one feeling out of place. After her first class, Nia had a long break before her next one. She considered going back to the dorm but decided against it. Zahara had teased her enough about being a homebody, and besides, she wanted to explore.

She wandered toward the student union, drawn by the smell of fresh coffee and the chatter of students. Inside, the atmosphere was lively. There were tables scattered across the main floor, some occupied by study groups and others by students enjoying snacks or playing card games.

Nia spotted a familiar face near the back—Taylor, sitting at a table with a group of other students. She caught Nia's eye and waved her over.

"Hey! Nia, right?" Taylor said as Nia approached. "Come join us."

Nia hesitated for a moment, but Taylor's smile was welcoming, and the other students didn't seem to mind. She slid into an empty seat and introduced herself to the group.

They were a mix of majors and backgrounds, and the conversation flowed easily. Nia learned that one of them, a tall guy named Elijah, was from a small town like hers, while another, a girl named Priya, was from the other side of the country.

"It's funny," Priya said. "No matter where you're from, the first week of college makes everyone feel like a fish out of water."

Nia nodded, feeling a sense of solidarity. Maybe she wasn't as out of place as she thought. By the time she got back to the dorm that afternoon, Nia was exhausted but in a good way. Zahara was sprawled on her bed, scrolling through her phone. She glanced up as Nia walked in.

"Look at you," Zahara said with a grin. "Out and about like a real college student."

Nia rolled her eyes, setting her bag down. "I met some people from my psych class. They were really nice."

"Good for you," Zahara said. "Told you this place wouldn't swallow you whole."

Nia smiled, sitting down on her bed. She pulled out her notebook and started jotting down notes from her first class, the words coming easily now that the initial nerves had faded.

"So," Zahara said after a moment, "what's next? You going to join a club or something?"

Nia shrugged. "Maybe. I haven't really thought about it."

"Well, think fast," Zahara said, tossing a flyer onto Nia's bed. "There's a club fair tomorrow. You should come with me."

Nia picked up the flyer, her curiosity piqued. "What clubs are you thinking of joining?"

"I'm keeping my options open," Zahara said with a wink. "But I heard there's a photography club, and I used to be pretty decent with a camera."

Nia raised an eyebrow. "You're full of surprises, aren't you?"

"Stick around, Maplegrove. I've got layers," Zahara said with a smirk

The next day, the campus was alive with energy for the club fair. Tables lined the quad, each one decorated with colorful signs and props meant to entice new members. Nia followed Zahara through the crowd, her eyes wide at the sheer variety of clubs on display.

"See anything you like?" Zahara asked, stopping at a table for the photography club.

"I'm not sure yet," Nia admitted, scanning the rows of tables.

Zahara handed her a flyer from the photography table. "Take your time. You'll know when you see it."

As they wandered, Nia found herself drawn to a table for the campus volunteer organization. The students behind the table were friendly, and their enthusiasm was infectious as they talked about their upcoming projects.

"This sounds amazing," Nia said, picking up a brochure.

"You should sign up," Zahara said, nudging her.

"I don't know..." Nia hesitated.

"Why not? You said you wanted to get out of your comfort zone, right?"

Nia sighed but couldn't argue with Zahara's logic. She added her name to the sign-up sheet and took a sticker with the club's logo.

That evening, Nia and Zahara sat in their room, comparing the flyers and brochures they'd collected.

"I can already tell you're going to be one of those overachievers with like ten clubs on your resume," Zahara teased.

"Not likely," Nia said with a laugh. "But I'm glad I signed up for something."

"See? You're already getting the hang of this college thing," Zahara said, stretching out on her bed.

Nia smiled, feeling a little more confident with each passing day. Maybe Zahara was right—maybe she was starting to find her place here.

She picked up her journal and opened it to a fresh page, her pen moving across the paper almost without thinking:

Day 3: I signed up for a club today. It's a small thing, but it feels like a step in the right direction. Maybe change isn't as scary as I thought.

The sun dipped lower in the sky as Nia and Zahara sat on the bench in the hidden garden, the golden light filtering through the leaves. They'd been quiet for a while now, each lost in her own thoughts.

Zahara broke the silence first, tilting her head toward Nia. "So, do you miss Maplegrove yet?"

Nia thought about the question carefully. Her first instinct was to say yes—it was home, after all. But as she looked around at the unfamiliar campus and felt the pull of something new and exciting, she realized her feelings were more complicated.

"Kind of," Nia said finally. "I miss knowing where I fit, you know? Back home, everything made sense. Here... I don't know. It's like trying to piece together a puzzle without knowing what the picture is supposed to look like."

Zahara nodded, her expression thoughtful. "Yeah, I get that. But sometimes the best puzzles are the ones where you don't see the picture coming together until the very end. It's frustrating as hell, but when you figure it out, it's worth it."

Nia smiled, her chest tightening at the unexpected wisdom in Zahara's words. "You're surprisingly philosophical for someone who uses her phone flashlight as a nightlight."

Zahara laughed, the sound bright and infectious. "Hey, don't knock it until you try it. Speaking of which, do you have any quirks I should know about? Like, are you secretly a sleep-talker or one of those people who keeps weird snacks under their bed?"

Nia pretended to think. "Hmm... I might have a stash of gummy bears in my desk drawer. But that's about as weird as it gets."

"Gummy bears? Weak. I was hoping for something scandalous, like a secret pet goldfish you smuggled in here," Zahara teased.

Nia chuckled. "Sorry to disappoint."

They sat in comfortable silence for a few more moments before Zahara stood and stretched. "Alright, let's head back before it gets dark. I don't trust myself to navigate this place at night even with my gift of direction."

Nia followed her out of the garden, feeling lighter somehow. For the first time since she'd arrived, she didn't feel so overwhelmed by everything. Back at the dorm, Nia tried to settle into a routine. She arranged her desk just the way she liked it, with her notebooks and pens in neat rows and her laptop angled perfectly toward her chair. She'd always found comfort in little things like that, even when everything else felt out of control.

Zahara, on the other hand, was the complete opposite. Her side of the room was a chaotic mess of clothes, books, and random items that made no sense together—like the guitar pick taped to her desk lamp and the half-eaten bag of chips under her bed.

"You know," Nia said as she watched Zahara dig through her

drawer for something, "your organizational system is... unique."

Zahara grinned, unbothered by the comment. "It's controlled chaos. I know exactly where everything is."

"Do you, though?"

"Of course. Watch this." Zahara reached into the drawer and pulled out a pair of socks, waving them triumphantly.

Nia rolled her eyes, but she couldn't help laughing. "I stand corrected."

"See? You've got to trust the process, Maplegrove," Zahara said, flopping onto her bed and kicking off her shoes.

Nia smiled to herself as she returned to her desk. It was moments like this—small, unremarkable exchanges—that made her feel like she might actually belong here.

That night, as Zahara scrolled through her phone and Nia flipped through the course syllabus for her psychology class, Zahara suddenly sat up.

"Hey, do you want to make a pact?"

Nia glanced at her, eyebrow raised. "A pact?"

"Yeah. Like a college survival pact. We both promise to get out of our comfort zones this year. Deal?" Zahara held out her pinky, a mischievous glint in her eye.

Nia hesitated. "What does 'out of our comfort zones' mean, exactly?"

"It means saying yes to things we'd normally say no to. Trying new stuff. Meeting new people. Living a little," Zahara said, her voice brimming with enthusiasm.

Nia bit her lip, considering it. She wasn't usually the type to make bold declarations or take risks, but something about Zahara's energy was contagious.

"Alright," Nia said, linking her pinky with Zahara's. "Deal."

"Perfect," Zahara said, flopping back onto her bed with a satisfied grin. "This is going to be the best year ever."

Nia wasn't sure about that, but as she lay in bed that night, staring at the ceiling, she felt a tiny flicker of excitement. Maybe Zahara was right. Maybe this year wouldn't just be about surviving—it could be about discovering who she was outside of Maplegrove. The next morning, Nia woke up early, her nerves already buzzing with anticipation for her first *real* day of classes. She dressed quickly, grabbed her backpack, and double-checked her schedule before heading out.

Zahara was still asleep, her arm flung dramatically over her face. Nia chuckled softly as she slipped out of the room, letting the door close quietly behind her.

The campus was alive with activity as students rushed to their classes. Nia found her way to the lecture hall for her Introduction to Psychology class, arriving with a few minutes to spare.

The room was massive, with rows of seats stretching up to the back wall. Nia chose a spot in the middle, hoping to blend in.

As the professor began the lecture, Nia pulled out her notebook, determined to focus. The material was fascinating—an overview of how the brain processes information and the ways humans perceive the world.

By the time the class ended, Nia felt energized. She'd always loved learning, and this class promised to challenge her in ways she hadn't expected. When Nia returned to the dorm later that afternoon, Zahara was sitting cross-legged on her bed, flipping through a magazine.

"How was it?" Zahara asked without looking up.

"Not bad," Nia said, setting her bag down. "The professor seems really smart, but not intimidating. I think I'm going to like it."

"Look at you, already geeking out about school," Zahara teased, but there was no malice in her tone. "I love to see it."

Nia rolled her eyes but smiled. "What about you? Any classes yet?"

"Not until tomorrow," Zahara said, tossing the magazine aside. "So today, I'm just vibing."

"Of course you are," Nia said with a laugh.

Chapter 2
First Day, First Doubts

Nia sat in the back of the large lecture hall, her notebook open but her mind racing. The professor, a middle-aged woman with sharp glasses and a no-nonsense attitude, was speaking at a pace that made Nia's head spin. It was the first *real* day of college, and it already felt like she was drowning.

Intro to psych was fine but this class's lecture was fast—so fast, in fact, that Nia could barely keep up. Her mind kept wandering to the people around her, students furiously taking notes, their pens flying across the pages. She felt like an outsider in a room full of people who already knew what they were doing, and she hadn't even figured out how to open her textbook yet.

"Everyone, please look up at the screen," the professor said, and Nia's eyes snapped back to the front. A slide filled with bullet points flashed up. Nia couldn't even process what was on the screen before it changed again. She scribbled down the key phrases she managed to catch, but they didn't make much sense to her.

What was she doing here?

She thought about Maplegrove. A small town where everyone

knew each other, where things felt slow and comfortable. She had been content there. But here, in this massive university, she felt completely out of place. The pace of the lecture, the vast amount of information being thrown at her, and the sense of competition in the room were all overwhelming.

By the time the professor wrapped up her introduction, Nia felt drained. She barely understood anything she'd written down. As the class filtered out, Nia lingered at her desk, trying to absorb the shock of it all. She felt her phone buzz in her pocket and pulled it out, hoping for a moment of comfort.

It was a text from Zahara:

Meet you at the quad in 10?

Nia stared at the screen for a moment, trying to gather her thoughts before she responded.

Sure, be there soon.

The walk to the quad was long, and Nia used the time to mentally prepare herself for the next part of the day. Her next class wasn't for another two hours, and she'd promised Zahara she would meet up with her after the second lecture.

When Nia arrived at the quad, she spotted Zahara immediately. She was sitting under a large tree, her sketchbook open on her lap, a marker in hand as she absentmindedly doodled.

"Hey," Nia said, approaching the tree.

Zahara looked up, a bright smile crossing her face. "Hey, you!" She closed her sketchbook, setting it aside. "How was the second lecture?"

Nia collapsed onto the grass beside Zahara, taking a deep breath. "It was... a lot. I don't even know if I understand half of what she said. I feel so out of place."

Zahara nodded sympathetically, but her smile remained steady. "Yeah, it can be overwhelming at first. You just have to trust that it'll get easier. You're here for a reason, right?"

Nia hesitated, biting her lip. "I guess. But I don't know. I mean everyone here seems so much more... capable. Like they know what they're doing. And I'm just trying to keep up."

Zahara's smile softened, and she placed a hand on Nia's shoulder. "Hey, everyone feels that way at first. You're not alone.

You just have to find your rhythm."

"I hope you're right," Nia murmured.

Just then, Nia's phone rang. It was her mom.

"Hey, Mom," Nia answered, sitting up straighter.

"How are the classes, sweetheart?" her mom asked, her voice full of warmth.

Nia forced a smile. "It was fine... just a lot of information all at once. I'm not sure I'm cut out for this, though."

"Cut out for what, honey?" her mom asked, her voice sounding concerned.

"I don't know... college. Everyone here seems so confident, and I feel like I'm falling behind already. I don't know if I belong."

There was a pause on the other end of the line before her mom responded, her tone gentle but firm. "Nia, you've always been capable. You're there for a reason, and you'll figure it out. Just give it time. College isn't supposed to feel easy at first."

"I don't know, Mom. I just feel like everyone here already has it together. I don't want to be the one who's always behind."

"You won't be," her mom said, her voice softening. "Just remember that you belong there as much as anyone else. I believe in you."

"Thanks, Mom," Nia said quietly.

Zahara, noticing the change in Nia's mood, leaned in and whispered, "Don't let it get to you, okay? You're doing fine."

Nia nodded, offering Zahara a small, grateful smile. "I'll try."

The rest of the day went by in a blur. Nia's next class was a general communications lecture, and it was just as overwhelming as the first. She could feel herself slipping further and further behind, her mind tangled in the rapid-fire explanations and the complex terminology the professor kept throwing out. By the time the class ended, Nia felt drained, her confidence even more shaken.

Zahara had invited Nia to an event that evening—some sort of student mixer for new students. Nia had hesitated at first, but Zahara insisted, pulling her along as the evening settled into a cooler air.

When they arrived, the event was packed, with music playing and students mingling in groups. The atmosphere was lively, and Nia could hear snippets of conversations as people introduced themselves and shared their excitement about the year ahead. Zahara, ever the social butterfly, jumped into the crowd effortlessly, drawing people in with her warm smile and quick wit.

Nia, however, found herself standing awkwardly at the edge of the group. She sipped her drink, trying to find a comfortable space to step into, but feeling more and more out of place. She watched as Zahara easily struck up conversations with other students, her easy confidence making Nia both envious and a little bit frustrated with herself.

"Hey, you look like you need some air."

The voice startled Nia, and she turned to see a tall man with deep brown hair and a caramel color complexion standing beside her.

"Hey I'm Jordan," he says giving a welcoming smile. "Hey, I'm Nia nice to meet you" Nia she says waving to him

"You okay?" he asked, looking concerned. "You don't look like you're having the time of your life."

Nia sighed. "I don't know, I just... this is a lot. Everyone here seems so sure of themselves, and I feel like I'm just trying to survive."

Jordan nodded, his expression softening. "I get it. But trust me, everyone feels that way at some point. College isn't a race. You'll find your groove, and when you do, it'll be worth it."

Nia nodded but didn't say anything else. Instead, she watched as Zahara continued to flit between conversations, talking to new faces with ease. She admired how confident Zahara was, and how naturally she connected with people.

As the evening wound down and people began to filter out of the event, Nia noticed something strange. She had been walking beside Jordan when they passed a quieter corner of the room. Zahara had pulled out her phone and was speaking softly to someone on the other end.

"Yeah, I know," Zahara said, her tone more serious than Nia

was used to hearing. "It's just... things are getting harder. You can't expect me to keep it together all the time."

Nia froze in place, not meaning to overhear, but hearing enough to feel the tension in Zahara's voice. Before she could react, Zahara quickly ended the call and slipped her phone back into her purse, her expression unreadable. Jordan and Nia looked at each other, confused and concerned, unsure of what to do next.

"Everything okay?" Nia asked, her voice cautious. "Not to intrude, but that sounded a bit stressful. You okay?"

Jordan's tone mirrored her concern, and he looked at Zahara with furrowed brows. Zahara's eyes flickered between them, her usual open demeanor now guarded. There was a brief pause before she responded. "Yeah, it's fine. I'll meet you back at the dorm, Nia."

Nia hesitated, watching Zahara for any signs of further distress. But Zahara's face was a mask of composure, the usual playful light in her eyes gone.

"Are you sure?" Nia asked, taking a step closer. "That didn't sound like everything was fine."

Zahara smiled weakly but didn't meet Nia's gaze. "I'm fine, really. Just... things with my family, you know? It's just a lot sometimes." She turned, her movements a little too quick, and began walking away.

Nia watched her leave, her chest tight. Zahara had always been the picture of calm confidence, the one who seemed to have everything under control. Seeing her like this made Nia feel uneasy like there was something more going on beneath the surface, something that Zahara wasn't ready to share.

"Don't worry too much," Jordan said, his voice quiet but reassuring. He stepped closer to Nia, giving her a gentle nudge. "I'm sure she's fine. She's strong."

Nia forced a smile, but it didn't quite reach her eyes. "Yeah... I guess. But it just didn't seem like her."

Jordan nodded, glancing after Zahara for a moment before focusing on Nia. "You're probably right. But sometimes people just need a little space to deal with things on their own."

"I hope so," Nia replied, her voice shakier than she intended.

"I'm going to head back to the dorm to check on her. Maybe we can catch up later?" She looked at Jordan, her heart still unsettled by the exchange.

"Most definitely!" Jordan said with a bright grin. "Here, take my number. Text me if you need anything, okay?" He fumbled for his phone and handed it to her, and Nia hesitated for just a second before typing in her number.

Jordan's smile grew as he pocketed his phone. "I'm looking forward to it. Don't let it get to you too much, Nia. We're all figuring it out."

"Thanks, Jordan," Nia said, managing a smile. "I really appreciate it."

They exchanged a quick hug, and then Nia watched him walk off into the crowd, disappearing into the throng of students. Nia stood there for a moment longer, the quiet of the room settling over her. Her mind kept circling back to Zahara, to the way she'd snapped back into her usual composure so quickly like she was trying to push something painful away.

With a sigh, Nia turned and made her way back to the dorm. Her thoughts felt heavy, weighing down her steps as she walked through the fading evening light. What had been a fun and distracting event just hours ago now seemed like a blur, the tension between Zahara and the phone call still fresh in Nia's mind.

Nia reached the dorm, but the elevator felt like it took forever to reach her floor. Her fingers drummed against the metal rail of the elevator as she stared at the rising numbers above the door. When it finally stopped, she stepped out and walked slowly to her room, feeling the weight of the unknown hanging around her. She reached the door to her room and paused, unsure of what to expect. Would Zahara be there? Would she want to talk about whatever was bothering her? Or would she shut herself off, like she seemed to be doing all night?

Nia opened the door quietly, the familiar smell of coffee and incense wafting through the air. She could hear the soft sound of music coming from the corner, and there, sitting cross-legged on the bed, was Zahara.

She looked up when Nia entered, a smile quickly flashing on her face, but it was faint and far too practiced. "Hey," Zahara said, setting down a book. She stood up, smoothing out her sweater. "You get back okay?"

Nia nodded but didn't move closer. "Yeah. Just wanted to check on you. I heard... I mean, I saw you talking to someone on the phone. You seemed upset. Are you sure you're okay?"

Zahara's eyes flickered to the side, and for a moment, Nia thought she saw something like fear in them. But it was gone almost instantly, replaced by a quick, forced smile. "It's nothing, really. Just... family stuff, you know? I'll be fine."

Nia bit her lip, not entirely convinced. She knew Zahara, knew how she could be so composed on the outside, even when things weren't perfect beneath the surface. She wasn't sure how much Zahara was keeping from her, but the wall she'd put up felt thicker now, more like a barrier than ever before.

"If you want to talk about it..." Nia started, but Zahara shook her head quickly.

"It's really fine, Nia. I don't want to drag you into my problems. Besides, we're here to enjoy the experience, right? Let's not let my family stuff ruin your first week." Zahara stepped toward Nia, putting a hand on her shoulder. "You okay?"

Nia nodded, though she wasn't sure. She glanced at Zahara, feeling that old sense of unease settle back in. But she couldn't push. Not now. Zahara had made it clear that she wasn't ready to talk.

"I'm okay," Nia said, though the words felt hollow.

Zahara smiled again, a little more genuinely this time. "Good. You know, we're in this together, right? Don't hesitate to ask if you need anything."

"Of course."

Nia lingered by the door for a moment longer, watching Zahara carefully. She could sense that something was off, but she didn't know how to help. The tension that had been so evident in Zahara's voice earlier still hung in the air, but Nia knew better than to push her too far.

"Goodnight, Zahara," Nia said finally, breaking the silence.

"Goodnight," Zahara replied, her voice soft.

She'd gotten no closer to understanding what was going on with Zahara, and now she wasn't sure if she even could. But she had the feeling that whatever Zahara was dealing with was far bigger than what Nia could help with. And that left her feeling more alone than she had in a long time.

As Nia lay in bed, staring at the ceiling, her thoughts shifted between the mysteries surrounding Zahara and the growing doubts about her own place in this new world. College was supposed to be the start of something exciting, right? Yet the more she tried to make sense of it, the more it all felt like it was slipping away from her.

Zahara's strange behavior had stayed with her all evening. Nia knew her well enough to recognize when something was wrong. She'd never been one to open up easily, but the Zahara she knew was always upbeat, always able to shake off whatever life threw at her. The Zahara she'd seen earlier, her voice strained and her movements quick, didn't match that image at all.

What's really going on with her?

Nia sighed, rubbing her eyes and trying to push the thought away. She couldn't keep worrying about Zahara when she had her own issues to sort through. The more she thought about her first lecture, the more she felt like she was losing her grip. It felt like everyone else was moving at full speed, while she was stuck, unsure of how to even take the first step. Was she really cut out for this? Could she handle this? And then, there were the doubts about whether she even belonged at this school in the first place.

Maybe Mom was right. Maybe I just need to give it time. But... how much time?

The more she thought about it, the more overwhelming everything felt. There was no clear path forward. She had no idea where she was going or how to get there. It felt like everyone else had a plan, a sense of purpose, while Nia was just trying to keep up.

She grabbed her phone, scrolling through her contacts, and stopping at Jordan's name. A wave of hesitation washed over her as she thought about texting him. The easy confidence he seemed to carry was both comforting and, a little intimidating. He seemed so calm, so sure of himself. Nia didn't know if she had the same confidence, but she couldn't shake the feeling that talking to someone might help clear her head. Maybe he would understand.

She tapped out a quick message.

Hey, Jordan, I know it's late, but do you mind if we talk for a bit?

She stared at the screen, her thumb hovering over the "send" button. What if he thought she was being silly or needy? What if he was already busy with something else? Nia quickly dismissed the thoughts.

I just need someone to talk to.

She pressed send, and a moment later, her phone buzzed with a response.

Of course. Want to meet up?

Nia couldn't help but smile. She quickly typed back.

Yeah, Meet you in 10.

She threw on her hoodie, grabbed her keys, and slipped out the door. The cool night air greeted her as she stepped into the hallway, the noise from the dorms muffled by the thick walls. She took the stairs instead of the elevator, needing to clear her mind with every step. Her thoughts were still a blur, a mix of her growing anxiety about school and the lingering worry about Zahara.

The campus was quiet at night, the only sounds coming from the rustling of leaves in the trees and the occasional distant laugh. Nia found Jordan sitting on a bench near the student center, his silhouette outlined by the soft glow of the streetlights. She sat beside him, her feet crunching on the gravel as she adjusted herself.

"You good?" Jordan asked, glancing at her.

Nia nodded, pulling her knees up to her chest. "Yeah, just... needed to get out of my head for a bit." She hesitated. "I don't know what I'm doing, Jordan. I feel so out of place here. The classes, the people, everything. It's like everyone has their lives figured out, and I'm just... floating."

Jordan shifted slightly, his posture relaxed but attentive. He didn't say anything for a few moments, giving her the space to continue.

"It's just so different from Maplegrove, you know?" Nia went on. "There, it felt like I was... part of something. But here, it's like I'm just trying to keep up. I can't even understand half of what they're teaching in class. And I keep looking around and thinking... maybe I don't belong here."

Jordan's eyes softened. "Nia, you're not the only one who feels that way." He ran a hand through his hair, sighing. "When I first started, I thought I was going to drown. There's so much pressure here, and it's easy to feel like you're not cut out for it. But you are. You're here for a reason. Just because things don't click right away doesn't mean you don't belong. It means you're still figuring it out, like everyone else."

"I don't know if I can handle it, though," Nia admitted, her voice barely above a whisper. "Every day, it feels harder to catch up. And then I see Zahara... I don't know what's going on with her, but I feel like I'm losing track of everything. Like I'm losing my sense of who I am."

Jordan was silent for a while, his eyes scanning the darkened campus around them. "Zahara's... complicated," he said finally, his voice thoughtful. "She's strong, but she's been through a lot. I think she's trying to handle everything on her own. But I wouldn't worry about her too much. You can't carry her burden too, Nia. You've got to take care of yourself."

"I know," Nia said quietly. "It's just... hard not to worry about her." She looked at Jordan. "You've been here longer than I have. How do you deal with everything? The pressure, the doubts... How do you keep going?"

Jordan met her gaze, his expression open but serious. "You just do. You take it one day at a time. College isn't about being perfect or figuring everything out all at once. You don't have to have it all together right now. You just have to keep going, even when you're not sure where you're headed." He paused, and his voice softened. "And sometimes you talk to people like I'm doing with you right now. It helps, even if it's just a little."

Nia smiled, feeling the warmth of his words settle in her chest.

"Thanks, Jordan. I needed to hear that."

Jordan grinned, his easy confidence shining through. "Anytime."

Nia sat in silence for a few moments, watching the stars twinkle above the campus, a sense of peace slowly settling over her. She still wasn't sure how everything would turn out, but for the first time that night, she didn't feel so alone. She had people who cared about her, and that was a start.

"Come on," Jordan said, standing up and offering her a hand. "I'm sure you've got a million things to think about, but maybe you could use a bit of a distraction. Let's go grab a late-night snack or something."

Nia took his hand and stood up, stretching. "Sounds good. I could use some comfort food."

As they walked back to the dorms, Nia felt lighter, as if the weight that had been pressing down on her had eased just a bit. She still had doubts, and still wasn't sure if she belonged here, but for now, she knew she wasn't facing it alone. And that made all the difference.

The walk back to the dorms was a quiet one, but not an uncomfortable silence. Nia felt a sense of calm she hadn't realized she needed. The gentle rhythm of their footsteps was grounding, and she found herself more present in the moment than she'd been all day. For a brief moment, the noise of her anxieties and insecurities faded into the background.

Jordan had a way of making everything seem a little more manageable. He didn't push her to talk about anything more than she was ready for, but he didn't let her feel like she was alone in her thoughts either. That balance was exactly what Nia needed right now.

As they reached the entrance of the dorm, Nia glanced at Jordan. "You sure you want to go grab something to eat? I don't want to keep you from whatever you were doing tonight."

Jordan gave her a teasing look as if the idea of leaving Nia alone to stew in her thoughts was the last thing on his mind. "Trust me, I wasn't doing anything important. And besides, I don't think you'd be able to survive college without learning about midnight snacks."

Nia smiled, the light teasing breaking through the last remnants of her tension. "I'll take your word for it."

They made their way to the cafeteria, which was still open at this late hour. It wasn't much, just a few vending machines and some leftover pizza from an earlier event, but it felt like the perfect comfort food. Nia wasn't particularly hungry, but something about the warmth of the place and the lack of pressure to be anywhere else helped her relax further.

"So," Jordan said, casually leaning against the vending machine as Nia grabbed a granola bar, "how was your classes?"

Nia grimaced slightly as she opened the wrapper. "It was... overwhelming. I couldn't keep up with everything. The pace is so fast, and the other students seem so confident. I just felt out of place. I keep thinking I might not be cut out for this."

Jordan tilted his head, studying her. "Everyone feels that way at first. I'm not saying it gets easier, but you get better at handling it. You have to learn how to manage everything. Time management, and stress management—those are the keys. It's a skill, and like any skill, you have to practice. But it's not impossible."

"I don't know if I even want to do all that," Nia admitted quietly, taking a small bite of the granola bar. "I keep doubting whether this is what I'm supposed to be doing. Maybe I'm not meant for college. I wasn't even sure I wanted to come here in the first place. It felt like something I was supposed to do, but I'm not sure anymore."

Jordan's expression softened. He pushed off from the vending machine and took a seat at one of the tables, motioning for Nia to join him. "I get that. The pressure to succeed here, to figure out your future right away—it's a lot to handle. But you don't have to have all the answers right now. Just focus on what feels right, one day at a time."

Nia sat down across from him, running her fingers over the edge of the table. "It's just so hard. I see people around me who know exactly what they want. Some of them are so sure of themselves. And then there's me, always second-guessing. I just want to feel like I belong here, like I'm doing the right thing."

"You belong here," Jordan said, his tone serious but kind. "You're not here by accident. You have as much of a right to be here as anyone else. It might not feel like it yet, but trust me, it will."

Nia looked at him, grateful for his words but unsure if she believed them. "But what if it never does? What if I don't ever feel like I belong?"

Jordan shrugged a gesture that was both casual and comforting. "I'm not going to lie to you. College can be tough. You'll have days where you question everything. But the trick is not letting those days define you. The struggle is part of it. It's how you grow. Don't let the bad days take away from the good ones. You have a chance to make this experience yours."

Nia chewed thoughtfully on the granola bar, her thoughts still a bit scattered. The idea of embracing the struggle wasn't something she had considered. It was hard to think about growth when she was so focused on feeling lost and uncertain. But Jordan had a point. Maybe she needed to take a step back and stop trying to have everything figured out right away.

"I think you're right," she said finally, her voice quieter than before. "I just have to stop being so hard on myself. It's just... hard to shake the feeling that I'm not enough."

Jordan gave her a pointed look. "Stop that. Don't measure yourself against others. Everyone's on their own journey. If you keep comparing yourself to others, you're always going to feel like you're falling short. Just focus on your own path. That's all anyone can ask of you."

Nia nodded slowly, feeling the truth in his words, even if she wasn't fully able to accept them yet. It would take time to let go of the comparison, but she knew he was right. Everyone had their own struggles, and it wasn't fair to constantly feel like she was behind because of how other people appeared to have it all together.

The two sat in companionable silence for a few moments, the hum of the vending machines and the soft murmur of distant voices filling the space. Nia felt lighter now than she had when she first walked in, and it wasn't just because of the granola bar. It was the feeling of connection, of not having to carry the weight of her doubts alone.

"I'm glad we talked," Nia said after a while, looking at Jordan. "I didn't realize how much I needed it."

Jordan smiled and stretched. "Anytime. Seriously. You don't have to figure everything out by yourself. We're all in this together, even if it doesn't always feel like it."

Nia returned his smile, feeling more at ease than she had in days. "Thanks, Jordan. I really mean it."

"Anytime," he repeated, rising from his seat. "Let's get some sleep before we get back into the chaos tomorrow."

Nia stood up with him, feeling a sense of gratitude for this unexpected friendship. Maybe the road ahead was still uncertain, but at least she had people to help her along the way.

As they made their way back to the dorm, Nia felt a little bit lighter, a little less burdened by the weight of her doubts. Tomorrow would come with its own challenges, but maybe, just maybe, she was starting to see a way forward. And that was enough for now.

The next day arrived with a quiet hum of anticipation that buzzed around Nia, despite her lingering doubts. She had barely gotten any sleep the night before, her mind buzzing with everything Jordan had said and the conversation she'd overheard with Zahara. The combination of all her emotions made her feel like she was walking on a tightrope, constantly teetering between hope and anxiety. But at least today, she had a little more clarity, a little more confidence.

She pulled herself out of bed, the morning light filtering through the blinds of her dorm room. The room, as sparsely decorated as it was, had started to feel a little more like her own space. The first few days had been filled with nerves and homesickness, but now, there was an odd comfort in the small corner she had claimed for herself. She threw on a hoodie and leggings, running a brush through her hair and glancing in the mirror. The reflection staring back at her wasn't perfect, but it was hers.

Just take it one step at a time, she reminded herself as she grabbed her bag and headed out the door.

Her first class of the day wasn't until late morning, so she had some time to kill before the whirlwind of lectures began again. She found herself standing in front of the student center, unsure of what to do with the time. There were small groups of students sitting on benches, some in deep conversation, others hunched over laptops, trying to finish last-minute assignments. She almost felt like an intruder in this busy world of higher education, but she couldn't help but be drawn to the energy, the quiet hum of life on campus.

As she walked across the quad, she spotted Jordan sitting by himself on one of the benches, scrolling through his phone. His easygoing presence was like a magnet, and Nia found herself gravitating toward him without even thinking. She smiled as she approached, and Jordan looked up, a grin spreading across his face when he saw her.

"Honestly, a little," Nia replied, easing herself down onto the bench beside him. "I think I'm starting to come to terms with the idea that it's okay not to have everything figured out. One step at a time, right?"

Jordan nodded, looking pleased. "Exactly. You can't expect to have it all together right away. That's what I was trying to say last night."

Nia paused for a moment, feeling the weight of the conversation she'd overheard with Zahara. She wasn't sure if it was the right time to bring it up, but something in her gut told her she couldn't ignore it.

"Jordan, I—" she began but hesitated. "I'm still a bit worried about Zahara. Hearing her on the phone, it sounds like she's dealing with something... tough. She didn't want to talk about it, but I could tell it's affecting her."

Jordan's expression shifted, a flicker of something crossing his face. It was brief, but Nia noticed it. "Yeah, it does sound like she's going through some things," he said quietly. "But you know her better than i do maybe she's just not great at opening up. I feel like she tries to handle everything on her own, but sometimes, it gets to be too much."

Nia frowned, a knot of concern tightening in her chest. "Maybe you're right i just hope she's ok?"

Jordan gave her a reassuring look, "I know you want to make sure Zahara is ok but you should just give her some time, I'm sure she will tell you everything eventually that's why I said you shouldn't worry too much".

Nia felt her heart tighten a little. She had always been the type to want to fix things for people she cared about, especially someone like Zahara, who had always seemed so strong and self-assured. But she also understood that there was only so much she could do.

"I just don't like seeing her like that," Nia said softly, more to herself than to Jordan. "She's always been the one who has it together."

Jordan smiled wryly, his tone lightening a bit. "You'll learn. Everyone has their struggles, even Zahara. She might seem invincible, but she's not. None of us are."

Nia nodded, taking in his words. It was hard to remember sometimes that everyone, even the people who seemed the most confident, had their battles. She couldn't carry Zahara's burdens for her, but she could be there, as a friend. That was all she could really do.

"Thanks, Jordan," Nia said, feeling a weight lift off her shoulders. "You always know how to make things seem less complicated."

He grinned. "It's what I do best."

The church bell rang, signaling the start of her first class. Nia glanced at her watch and stood up, brushing off her leggings. "I guess I should get going. Thanks for the talk, Jordan. Really. I feel a lot better."

Jordan stood up as well. "No problem. We'll talk more later, okay?"

"Definitely," Nia said, giving him a small smile before turning to walk toward the lecture halls.

As she stepped into the classroom, the familiar sense of nervousness crept back in. The desks were arranged in neat rows, and the professor was already setting up his materials at the front of the room. Nia took a seat near the back, hoping to fade into the background. But as more students filed in, she realized that the pressure she had been feeling the day before was still there. She wasn't sure what to expect from this class, but the same doubts returned: *What if I'm not prepared? What if I fall behind?*

She opened her notebook, the scratch of the pen against the paper grounding her, and tried to breathe through the unease. Maybe it wasn't so much about feeling ready; maybe it was just about showing up.

The lecture began, and for the first time that day, Nia was able to focus entirely on what the professor was saying. His voice was calm, the material engaging. It wasn't easy, but it was easier than she had anticipated. As the class went on, Nia found herself making connections and understanding more than she had thought possible.

By the time the class ended, she felt a small sense of accomplishment. She wasn't all the way there yet, but this was progress. She had made it through the lecture, and she had actually understood most of it.

Walking out of the classroom, Nia felt the smallest spark of hope, a flicker of belief that maybe—just maybe—she could do this after all. The road ahead wouldn't be easy, but it was hers to walk, one step at a time.

And maybe, just maybe, she was starting to find her place here.

Chapter 3
Navigating the Unknown

The sun filtered through the sheer curtains in Nia's dorm room, casting a golden glow over her neatly made bed and the half-unpacked boxes shoved into the corner. She had woken up earlier than expected, jolted by the buzz of her phone. It was a message from Zahara: "Hey, let's grab breakfast together this morning. Meet me at the dining hall at 8?"

Rubbing the sleep from her eyes, Nia glanced at the time—7:15 a.m. It was early for a college student's standards, but Zahara rarely reached out first. Maybe the tension Nia had felt between them was starting to loosen. After a quick shower and throwing on some jeans and her favorite hoodie, Nia grabbed her bag and headed out.

The morning air was crisp, and the campus buzzed with students heading to their classes, chatting in groups, or clutching coffee cups like lifelines. Spotting Zahara sitting at an outdoor table near the dining hall, her curly hair catching the sunlight like a halo, Nia waved.

"Hey," she called as she approached. Zahara looked up, a small smile tugging at her lips. "Hey yourself. You're early."

"You said 8, and it's... 7:58," Nia said with a smirk, dropping her bag onto the chair and sitting across from Zahara.

"Pretty on time, if you ask me." Zahara chuckled, but the laughter didn't quite reach her eyes. "Fair enough. Let's grab some food before the rush starts."

The dining hall was quieter than expected. They each grabbed trays, filling them with scrambled eggs, fruit, and toast. Zahara opted for black coffee, while Nia chose orange juice. Once seated, Zahara picked at her food, her fork idly moving pieces of egg around her plate.

"You doing okay?" Nia asked gently after a few moments of silence. Zahara glanced up, her expression neutral.

"Yeah, just... tired, I guess. Classes are already a lot, you know?"

"I get it," Nia said softly. "But if you ever want to talk about it, I'm here."

For a moment, Zahara seemed like she might open up, but instead, she shrugged.

"Thanks, Nia. I appreciate it."

The rest of breakfast passed with light conversation. They discussed classes, professors, and Zahara's latest obsession with a true-crime podcast. Nia laughed at Zahara's witty commentary, but she couldn't shake the feeling that her friend was holding something back. As they walked out of the dining hall, Zahara checked her phone.

"I've got a class in fifteen minutes, so I should head out. But thanks for coming to breakfast. It was nice to catch up."

"Anytime," Nia said, watching Zahara walk away.

Something was definitely off, but Nia knew better than to push. Zahara would talk when she was ready—or at least, Nia hoped she would.

Later that afternoon, Nia found herself in the library, her laptop open and her fingers poised over the keyboard. Her first big assignment was due in two weeks, and though she'd told herself she'd get a head start, her mind kept drifting. The library was quiet, save for the occasional rustle of papers or the soft tapping of keyboards. She glanced around, hoping for a distraction, and spotted Leila, her groupmate from their class project, seated at a nearby table surrounded by books. Nia hesitated, then stood and walked over.

"Hey, Leila." Leila looked up, her face breaking into a warm smile.

"Oh, hey! Nia, right?"

"Yeah. Mind if I join you?"

"Not at all," Leila said, gesturing to the chair across from her.

"How's it going?" "Trying to make sense of this assignment," Nia admitted, sitting down and opening her notebook. "It feels like everyone else in class knows what they're doing, and I'm just... floundering."

Leila laughed softly. "Trust me, you're not alone. I'm still adjusting to how different college is from high school. And being so far from home doesn't make it any easier."

"Where's home for you?" Nia asked.

"Egypt," Leila said, her eyes lighting up. "Cairo, to be exact. It's beautiful there—busy, vibrant, and full of life. But it's... different here. Quieter, for one. And I miss my family."

"I can't imagine being that far away," Nia said. "I mean, I miss my family, and they're only a few hours away. How do you handle it?"

Leila shrugged, her smile tinged with sadness. "Some days are harder than others. But I remind myself why I'm here—to learn, to grow, to create opportunities for myself. It helps to stay focused on the bigger picture."

Nia nodded, feeling a pang of guilt for how much she'd been second-guessing her decision to be here. If Leila could navigate college while being thousands of miles from home, Nia could certainly handle her own challenges.

"Thanks, Leila," Nia said after a moment. "I needed to hear that."

Leila smiled. "Anytime. And hey, if you ever need help with the project, let me know. I'm pretty good at research."

"Deal," Nia said, feeling a little more grounded than she had before.

That evening, Nia returned to her dorm, her backpack slung over one shoulder and her mind buzzing with thoughts from the day. She unlocked the door to find Zahara lying on her bed, headphones in and eyes closed.

"Hey," Nia said, setting her bag down. Zahara opened her eyes and pulled out one earbud.

"Hey. How was your day?"

"Not bad," Nia said, sitting on the edge of her bed. "I ran into Leila at the library. We talked for a while. She's really nice."

"She is," Zahara agreed, though her tone was distracted.

Nia hesitated, then asked, "How was your day?"

Zahara sat up, stretching. "Busy. Classes, meetings, all that. You know how it is."

Nia wanted to press further, to ask if Zahara was really okay, but she held back. Instead, she changed the subject. "Jordan mentioned a movie night happening on campus this weekend. You want to go?"

"Maybe," Zahara said, a small smile tugging at her lips.

"What movie?"

"Something cheesy, probably," Nia said with a laugh. "But it could be fun."

"Yeah, we'll see," Zahara said, lying back down.

Nia watched her for a moment, then turned to her own work. Whatever was going on with Zahara, Nia hoped she'd feel comfortable sharing eventually. For now, all she could do was be there—and maybe try to make her laugh with a cheesy movie night

As the days passed, Nia found herself settling into a rhythm. Classes were still challenging, but she was learning how to keep up. Her group project with Leila and Chris was off to a decent start, and she was starting to feel like she could actually contribute something meaningful. Jordan continued to be a steady presence in her life, always ready with a joke or a piece of advice. And though Zahara remained guarded, their breakfasts together became a regular occurrence, a quiet routine that grounded Nia in the midst of her chaotic new world. It wasn't perfect, and she still had moments of doubt, but Nia was beginning to believe that maybe she could handle this after all. College was an unknown labyrinth of challenges and opportunities, but she was learning how to navigate it—one step at a time.

The next morning started with the sound of Nia's alarm clock blaring. She groaned, fumbling to silence it, and rolled out of bed, her body protesting every step toward the shower. It was Thursday, the last hurdle before the weekend, but Nia didn't feel like she was anywhere near the finish line. Her first lecture of the day was a communication class that started at 8 a.m., and with the pressure of staying ahead, Nia couldn't afford to miss it. By the time she left the dorm, Zahara was still asleep, curled under her blanket like a cocoon. Nia paused, wondering if she should wake her, but decided against it. Zahara's schedule was different from hers, and after the tension earlier in the week, Nia didn't want to overstep.

The walk across campus was brisk, the autumn air sharp but refreshing. Students bustled in every direction, bundled in jackets and scarves, clutching coffee cups as they hurried to their classes. Nia couldn't help but feel like just another face in the crowd, anonymous and insignificant. It was both freeing and unsettling at the same time. When she finally reached the lecture hall, she slid into her usual seat near the middle, pulling out her notebook and laptop. Leila waved to her from a row over, a bright smile on her face.

"Morning," Leila mouthed, and Nia waved back, grateful for the friendly gesture.

The lecture was as dense and fast-paced as ever. The professor spoke in rapid-fire sentences, barely pausing to breathe as he covered slides filled with diagrams and terminology. Nia typed as fast as she could, her notes a chaotic mix of bullet points and half-formed sentences. She glanced at the students around her, noticing how some of them seemed completely at ease, nodding along like they already understood everything. It was hard not to feel out of place like she was the only one struggling to keep up.

After class, Leila caught up with her as they exited the building. "That was intense," Leila said, her voice tinged with a mix of exhaustion and amusement. "Did you catch what he said about communication in crisis situations? Because who knew talking to each other could be so complicated."

Nia laughed, feeling a bit lighter. "Barely. I think I got half of it, but the rest? No clue. We should probably go over it before the quiz next week."

"Definitely," Leila agreed. "Want to meet up this weekend to study? Maybe Saturday afternoon?"

"Yeah, that sounds good," Nia said. "Thanks, Leila."

"No problem. We're all in this together, right?" Leila flashed another warm smile before heading off to her next class.

As Nia walked back across campus, she felt a flicker of hope. Maybe she wasn't as alone in this as she thought. Leila's kindness and willingness to help made her feel like she was starting to find her footing, even if only a little.

Back at the dorm later that afternoon, Nia found Zahara sitting at her desk, headphones in and eyes glued to her laptop screen. She was so focused that she didn't even notice Nia come in until she dropped her bag onto her bed. "Hey," Zahara said, pulling out her earbuds. "How was class?"

"Still Intense," Nia said, kicking off her shoes and flopping onto her bed. "But I survived. How about you?"

Zahara hesitated for a moment before shrugging. "Same old. Meetings, assignments, trying to stay on top of everything."

Nia sat up, watching her friend closely. "You sure you're okay? You've seemed... off lately."

Zahara sighed, leaning back in her chair. "I'm fine, Nia. Really. Just a lot on my plate right now."

"Okay," Nia said, though she didn't entirely believe her. "If you ever want to talk about it, you know I'm here, right?"

"I know," Zahara said, offering a small smile. "Thanks."

The rest of the afternoon passed quietly. Nia worked on her communication notes, trying to make sense of the lecture, while Zahara alternated between typing furiously on her laptop and scrolling through her phone. The silence wasn't uncomfortable, but it wasn't entirely easy either. There was a weight in the air, unspoken but present, and Nia couldn't shake the feeling that Zahara was keeping something from her.

Later that evening, Nia received a text from Jordan: *Movie night's still on for tomorrow. Are you and Zahara coming?*

Nia hesitated before replying: *I'll be there. Not sure about Zahara, though. She's been busy lately.*

Jordan's response came almost immediately: *Bring her if you can. Could be good for her.*

She didn't want to push her friend, but maybe Jordan was right. A night out could be exactly what Zahara needed.

"Hey," Nia said, looking over at Zahara. "Jordan's hosting a movie night tomorrow. You should come. It'll be fun."

Zahara glanced up from her laptop, her expression unreadable. "I don't know. I've got a lot to do."

"It's Friday night," Nia said. "You deserve a break. Come on, it'll be good to get out of here for a bit."

Zahara hesitated, her fingers tapping lightly on the edge of her desk. Finally, she sighed. "Okay. But only if it's not some awful rom-com."

Nia grinned. "Deal."

The next day passed quickly, with classes and group meetings keeping Nia busy until the early evening. By the time she returned to the dorm to get ready for the movie night, Zahara was already dressed, wearing a casual but stylish outfit that made Nia feel underdressed in her hoodie and jeans. "You look great," Nia said, grabbing her jacket.

"Thanks," Zahara said, her tone light. "Ready to go?"

The movie night was held in one of the larger common rooms on campus, with a projector set up and bean bags and blankets scattered across the floor. The smell of popcorn filled the air, and students milled about, chatting and laughing as they found spots to sit. Jordan waved them over as soon as they walked in, grinning from ear to ear. "You made it!" he said, pulling Nia into a quick hug. "And you brought Zahara! Awesome."

Zahara smiled politely, her eyes scanning the room. "Nice setup," she said.

"Thanks," Jordan said, leading them to a spot near the front. "We're starting with something light—an action-comedy. No rom-coms, I promise."

The movie started, and for a while, Nia allowed herself to relax. She laughed at the jokes, munched on popcorn, and stole glances at Zahara, who seemed to be enjoying herself, even if she wasn't as animated as usual. Jordan sat next to them, cracking jokes and offering running commentary that made Nia laugh even harder.

But as the night wore on, Nia noticed Zahara checking her phone more frequently, her expression growing tenser with each glance. When the movie ended and people began to gather their things, Zahara stood abruptly. "I'm going to head back," she said, avoiding Nia's gaze.

"Already?" Nia asked, standing up. "Are you okay?"

"Yeah, just tired," Zahara said quickly. "Thanks for inviting me, though. It was fun."

Before Nia could say anything else, Zahara slipped out of the room, leaving Nia standing there, confused and worried. Jordan walked up beside her, his brow furrowed. "She okay?" he asked.

"I don't know," Nia admitted. "Something's been bothering her, but she won't talk about it."

Jordan nodded, his expression thoughtful. "Just give her some space. She'll come around when she's ready."

"Yeah," Nia said, though the knot in her stomach didn't ease. As she walked back to her dorm that night, the campus quiet under the glow of streetlights, Nia couldn't shake the feeling that something was wrong—and that whatever it was, Zahara was dealing with it alone.

The weekend brought a brief reprieve from the usual chaos of classes and assignments, but Nia found herself unable to fully relax. Zahara's sudden departure from the movie night lingered in her mind, gnawing at her with a persistent sense of unease. It wasn't like Zahara to shut people out completely, at least not like this. The two of them had grown close quickly, and Zahara's guarded demeanor now felt like a wall that Nia wasn't sure how to climb.

By Saturday afternoon, Nia was seated at a small table in the campus library, her communication notes spread out in front of her. She was supposed to be meeting Leila for their study session, but her mind kept drifting. The quiet hum of the library and the faint scratching of pens from other students didn't do much to drown out her thoughts. She couldn't help but wonder what Zahara might be dealing with—whether it was family issues, school stress, or something deeper. Nia had tried to respect her space, but she was starting to feel like maybe she wasn't doing enough to help.

"Hey!" Leila's cheerful voice broke through Nia's thoughts. She looked up to see her study partner approaching, a tote bag slung over one shoulder and an iced coffee in her hand. "Sorry, I'm late. The line at the café was ridiculous."

"No worries," Nia said, trying to muster a smile. She gestured to the seat across from her. "Ready to tackle the wonderful world of communication in crisis?"

Leila groaned as she sat down. "Barely. I've been trying to go over the material all morning, and my brain is fried. I swear, social science is just a cruel joke sometimes."

The two of them dove into their notes, quizzing each other and trying to make sense of the dense material. For a while, Nia managed to push her worries aside and focus on the task at hand. Leila's upbeat energy was contagious, and Nia found herself laughing more than she expected to. But even in the midst of their studying, her thoughts kept drifting back to Zahara.

"You okay?" Leila asked at one point, giving Nia a curious look. "You seem a little distracted."

Nia hesitated, debating whether to bring it up. "Yeah, I'm fine," she said after a moment. "Just... my roommate's been acting kind of weird lately. I'm worried about her."

Leila nodded, her expression softening. "That sucks. Is she the type to open up about stuff, or does she keep it bottled up?"

"The latter," Nia admitted. "I've tried to ask her if she's okay, but she just brushes it off. I don't want to push her, but... I don't know. It's hard to just sit back and do nothing."

"That's tough," Leila said. "Maybe she just needs time. But if you're really worried, maybe you could try finding a way to connect with her that doesn't feel like prying. Sometimes people just need to know someone's there for them, you know?"

"Yeah," Nia said, mulling over Leila's words. She appreciated the advice, even if it didn't provide an immediate solution. "Thanks."

Leila smiled. "Anytime. Now, let's get back to this. I refuse to let this defeat me."

After their study session, Nia returned to the dorm to find Zahara sitting on her bed, scrolling through her phone. She looked up when Nia walked in, her expression unreadable. "Hey," Zahara said, her voice neutral.

"Hey," Nia replied, setting her bag down. She hesitated, wondering if she should bring up what was on her mind, but decided against it. Instead, she said, "How's your day been?"

"Fine," Zahara said with a shrug. "Just catching up on some stuff."

Nia nodded, unsure of how to continue the conversation. The tension between them felt palpable, and she hated it. She wanted things to go back to the way they had been before when Zahara had been more open and their conversations had felt easy. But now, everything felt guarded and fragile.

Later that evening, Nia found herself texting Jordan. *Hey, any chance you're free to hang out?*

His response came quickly: *Sure. Meet me at the student center in 20?*

Grateful for the distraction, Nia grabbed her jacket and headed out. The student center was buzzing with activity when she arrived, students scattered across couches and tables, chatting and studying. Jordan was waiting near the entrance, his easy smile immediately putting Nia at ease.

"Hey," he said, pulling her into a quick hug. "What's up?"

Nia sighed, running a hand through her hair. "Just needed to get out of the dorm for a bit. Zahara's been acting weird, and I don't know what to do about it."

Jordan nodded, his expression thoughtful. "Yeah, I noticed she seemed off last night. Did something happen?"

"Not really," Nia said. "She's just been... distant. And when I try to talk to her about it, she brushes me off."

"Maybe she's dealing with something personal," Jordan suggested. "Sometimes people just need space, you know?"

"I know," Nia said. "I just feel like I should be doing more to help. But I don't even know where to start."

Jordan gave her a reassuring smile. "You're a good friend, Nia. Just keep being there for her. She'll come around when she's ready."

They spent the next hour talking about everything and nothing, and by the time Nia returned to the dorm, she felt a little lighter. But when she walked into the room, Zahara was gone. Her bed was neatly made, and her laptop and books were stacked on her desk. A folded piece of paper sat on Nia's pillow.

Frowning, Nia picked up the note and unfolded it. The handwriting was neat but rushed.

Hey Nia,
Went out for a bit. Don't wait up.
—Zahara

The note didn't offer much information, but it left Nia with a sinking feeling in her stomach. She set it down on her desk and sat on the edge of her bed, staring at the blank walls of their dorm room. She didn't know where Zahara had gone or when she'd be back, but the thought of her friend wandering around campus alone late at night didn't sit right with her.

Hours passed, and Zahara still didn't return. Nia eventually climbed into bed, her mind racing with questions and worries. She wanted to believe Zahara was fine, that she was just blowing off steam or clearing her head, but the doubt gnawed at her. When she finally fell asleep, her dreams were restless and filled with fragmented images of Zahara walking away, always just out of reach.

The next morning, Zahara returned as if nothing had happened. She walked in carrying a coffee cup and wearing the same clothes as the night before, her expression calm and composed. "Morning," she said, setting her coffee down on her desk.

"Morning," Nia replied, watching her carefully. "You okay?"

"Yeah," Zahara said casually. "Just needed some air last night."

Nia wanted to press her for more details, but the look on Zahara's face made her stop. She recognized the guarded expression, the way Zahara's shoulders were just slightly tense. Whatever Zahara was dealing with, she wasn't ready to share it. Nia nodded, deciding to let it go for now.

But as Zahara sat down at her desk and opened her laptop, Nia couldn't shake the feeling that this was only the beginning of something much bigger—something that would eventually force its way into the open, whether Zahara was ready for it or not.

Nia woke up the next morning feeling restless, her thoughts immediately circling back to Zahara. Her roommate had come back late the night before, acting as if nothing was amiss. The calm, almost too-casual demeanor Zahara displayed only deepened Nia's concerns. She wanted to respect Zahara's privacy, but her intuition told her something was wrong. Still, Nia decided to give her friend space for now, hoping that Zahara would come to her when she was ready.

The day ahead was packed with classes, starting with a grueling psychology lecture that left Nia feeling mentally drained. She trudged across campus afterward, her backpack weighing heavily on her shoulders, both physically and metaphorically. The vibrant fall leaves fluttered in the wind, their colors brilliant against the crisp blue sky, but Nia barely noticed. Her mind was preoccupied with Zahara, and it didn't help that she still felt like she was barely keeping her own head above water when it came to her coursework. College was starting to feel like a maze she couldn't quite navigate.

During lunch, Nia met up with Leila and Chris in the bustling dining hall. Leila waved her over-enthusiastically, while Chris offered a subdued nod. Nia slid her tray onto the table and sat down, grateful for the distraction.

"So, how's everyone doing on the group project?" Leila asked, biting into a sandwich. "Because I, for one, am still trying to figure out how to even start the research."

Chris sighed, pushing his salad around on his plate. "I've been chipping away at it, but honestly, it feels like we're reinventing the wheel with this professor's expectations."

Nia managed a small smile. "Same here. I've been so swamped with everything else that I haven't had a chance to really dive into it."

"Well, no pressure," Leila said brightly. "We'll get through it together. And if worse comes to worst, we can always bribe the professor with cookies."

Chris snorted. "If only it were that easy."

As the conversation shifted to lighter topics, Nia felt herself relax a little. She appreciated how Leila's humor and Chris's dry wit balanced each other out, making the group dynamic oddly enjoyable despite the stress of their project. For a while, Nia was able to set her worries about Zahara aside and focus on the here and now.

But later that afternoon, as she was walking back to her dorm, she spotted Zahara sitting alone on a bench near the campus quad. Zahara's head was bowed, her fingers tapping absentmindedly against the edge of her phone. She looked distant, her usually confident posture replaced by a slump that made her seem smaller somehow.

Nia hesitated for a moment, then walked over. "Hey," she said softly, taking a seat beside Zahara. "You okay?"

Zahara looked up, her expression briefly startled before she masked it with a small smile. "Hey, Nia. Yeah, I'm fine. Just... thinking."

"Want to talk about it?" Nia offered, her tone gentle.

Zahara shook her head. "Not really. It's nothing serious, just some stuff on my mind."

Nia studied her friend, unsure of whether to push further. She decided to let it go, at least for now. "Okay. Just know I'm here if you need to talk."

"Thanks," Zahara said quietly, her gaze drifting to the leaves scattered across the ground.

They sat in silence for a while, the sounds of campus life humming around them. Students hurried past, their laughter and chatter filling the air, but it felt like Nia and Zahara were in their own little bubble of stillness. Nia wanted to do more, to say the right thing that would make Zahara open up, but she didn't know how. All she could do was be there.

That evening, back in their dorm, Zahara seemed a little more at ease. She joined Nia in watching a Netflix movie, laughing at the ridiculous plot and making sarcastic comments that reminded Nia of the Zahara she had first met. It was a small step, but it gave Nia hope that things might eventually get back to normal.

The next few days passed in a blur of classes, assignments, and group project meetings. Nia threw herself into her studies, partly to keep up with the demanding coursework and partly to distract herself from her worries about Zahara. She and Leila worked late into the night one evening, poring over research articles and brainstorming ideas for their project. Chris joined them for a while, his usual cynicism softened by a surprising level of insight that made Nia appreciate him even more.

But despite her busy schedule, Nia couldn't shake the feeling that Zahara was keeping something important from her. The thought gnawed at her, making it hard to focus completely. She found herself watching Zahara more closely, looking for clues in her behavior that might explain what was going on.

One night, Nia woke up to the sound of muffled voices. She sat up in bed, blinking groggily in the dim light. Across the room, Zahara was sitting on her bed, her phone pressed to her ear. Her voice was low, but the tension in her tone was unmistakable.

"I'm doing the best I can," Zahara was saying. "You don't have to remind me how hard this is."

There was a pause, during which Nia could hear the faint murmur of the person on the other end of the call. Zahara's shoulders tensed, and she rubbed her forehead in frustration. "I know. But I can't keep fixing everything. It's too much."

Nia debated whether to pretend she was still asleep or to let

Zahara know she was awake. Before she could decide, Zahara ended the call with a terse "I'll figure it out" and tossed her phone onto the bed. She sat there for a moment, staring at the wall, before burying her face in her hands.

"Zahara?" Nia said softly, her voice breaking the silence.

Zahara looked up, startled. Her eyes flicked to Nia, and for a moment, she seemed to debate whether to say anything. Then she sighed, her shoulders slumping. "Sorry if I woke you."

"It's okay," Nia said, sitting up fully. "You don't have to tell me what's going on, but... I'm here if you need to talk."

For a long moment, Zahara didn't say anything. Then, finally, she spoke, her voice barely above a whisper. "It's my family. Things have been... complicated. My parents are going through a divorce, and I've been caught in the middle of it. They keep asking me to mediate like I'm some kind of referee. It's exhausting."

Nia's heart ached for her friend. "That sounds really hard," she said gently. "I'm sorry you're dealing with that."

Zahara nodded, her expression weary. "It is. And on top of that, I'm trying to keep up with classes and everything else. It just feels like too much sometimes."

"I get it," Nia said. "And you don't have to go through it alone. I'm here for you, okay? Whatever you need."

Zahara gave her a small, grateful smile. "Thanks, Nia. That means a lot."

They sat in silence for a while, the weight of Zahara's confession hanging between them. Nia felt a surge of determination—she didn't know how, but she was going to help her friend through this, no matter what it took.

The next morning, the dorm felt quieter than usual. Zahara's admission the night before hung heavily in the air, and though Nia didn't want to push, she also couldn't pretend everything was fine. She watched Zahara move through their shared space with quiet efficiency, brushing her hair and packing her bag like any other day, but there was an added weight to her movements. Zahara seemed more withdrawn, her gaze unfocused as she tied her shoes at the foot of her bed.

"You have class soon?" Nia asked, breaking the silence.

"Yeah," Zahara replied without looking up. "Chemistry in fifteen."

Nia hesitated, fiddling with the strap of her bag. "Do you want to grab coffee after? I'm free around noon."

Zahara glanced at her, a flicker of surprise in her eyes, but she nodded. "Yeah, sure. That sounds nice."

It was a small win, but Nia clung to it as she headed to her own class. The morning passed in a blur of lectures and note-taking, but she found herself checking the clock frequently, counting down the minutes until her meeting with Zahara. When noon finally rolled around, she hurried to the campus café, her stomach fluttering with a mix of nerves and determination.

Zahara was already there, sitting at a small table by the window with her hands wrapped around a cup of tea. She looked up as Nia approached, offering a faint smile. "Hey."

"Hey," Nia said, sliding into the seat across from her. She set her coffee down and took a deep breath. "Thanks for meeting me."

"Of course," Zahara said, her tone light but guarded. "What's up?"

Nia hesitated, searching for the right words. "I just... I wanted to check-in. I know you've been dealing with a lot, and I want to make sure you're okay."

Zahara's smile faltered, and she looked down at her cup. "I appreciate that, Nia. I really do. But I don't want to drag you into my problems. It's not fair to you."

"It's not dragging me into anything," Nia said firmly. "You're my friend, Zahara. I care about you. And if you need someone to talk to or even just someone to sit with, I'm here."

For a moment, Zahara didn't respond. She stared out the window, her expression distant, before finally speaking. "It's just hard, you know? My parents have always been so... intense. They expect so much from me, and now, with the divorce, it feels like I'm being pulled in two different directions. They don't realize how much it's affecting me. Or maybe they do, and they just don't care."

Nia's chest tightened. "I'm so sorry, Zahara. That sounds incredibly overwhelming."

"It is," Zahara admitted. "And I keep telling myself I should be able to handle it. I mean, I've always been the strong one, the responsible one. But lately, it feels like I'm cracking under the pressure."

"You don't have to handle it alone," Nia said gently. "It's okay to lean on people sometimes. That doesn't make you any less strong."

Later that afternoon, Nia found herself back in the library, working on the group project with Leila and Chris. The three of them had settled into a productive rhythm, bouncing ideas off each other and making steady progress. Leila's enthusiasm kept the mood light, while Chris's analytical approach helped them stay on track.

"So, how's Zahara doing?" Leila asked during a brief lull in their work. "You mentioned she was having a tough time."

Nia glanced around, lowering her voice. "She's... opening up a bit. It's been hard for her, but I think she's starting to let me in."

"That's good," Leila said with a nod. "Sometimes just knowing someone's there for you can make a huge difference."

Chris, who had been quietly typing on his laptop, spoke up unexpectedly. "If she needs more support, you could always suggest the counseling center. I know a lot of people who've found it helpful."

Nia considered this. She hadn't thought about the counseling center before, but it might be a good resource for Zahara. "I'll mention it to her if she seems open to it. Thanks, Chris."

He shrugged, his expression neutral. "No problem. College can be rough. Everyone needs help sometimes."

As the study session wrapped up, Nia felt a renewed sense of purpose. She couldn't fix everything for Zahara, but she could be there for her and encourage her to seek the help she needed. It was a start.

That evening, back in the dorm, Nia brought up the idea of the counseling center. She approached it cautiously, not wanting to push Zahara too hard. "Hey, I was talking to some friends today, and they mentioned the counseling center on campus. Have you ever thought about checking it out?"

Zahara looked at her, and for the first time, Nia saw tears glistening in her eyes. She quickly blinked them away, but the vulnerability in her expression was undeniable. "Thanks, Nia. That means a lot."

They sat in comfortable silence for a while, sipping their drinks and watching the world go by outside the café window. Nia felt a sense of relief knowing that Zahara had opened up, even just a little. It was a step forward, and she was determined to support her friend however she could.

Later that afternoon, Nia found herself back in the library, working on the group project with Leila and Chris. The three of them had settled into a productive rhythm, bouncing ideas off each other and making steady progress. Leila's enthusiasm kept the mood light, while Chris's analytical approach helped them stay on track.

"So, how's Zahara doing?" Leila asked during a brief lull in their work. "You mentioned she was having a tough time."

Nia glanced around, lowering her voice. "She's... opening up a bit. It's been hard for her, but I think she's starting to let me in."

"That's good," Leila said with a nod. "Sometimes just knowing someone's there for you can make a huge difference."

Chris, who had been quietly typing on his laptop, spoke up unexpectedly. "If she needs more support, you could always suggest the counseling center. I know a lot of people who've found it helpful."

Nia considered this. She hadn't thought about the counseling center before, but it might be a good resource for Zahara. "I'll mention it to her if she seems open to it. Thanks, Chris."

He shrugged, his expression neutral. "No problem. College can be rough. Everyone needs help sometimes."

As the study session wrapped up, Nia felt a renewed sense of purpose. She couldn't fix everything for Zahara, but she could be there for her and encourage her to seek the help she needed. It was a start.

That evening, back in the dorm, Nia brought up the idea of the counseling center. She approached it cautiously, not wanting to push Zahara too hard. "Hey, I was talking to some friends today, and they mentioned the counseling center on campus. Have you ever thought about checking it out?"

Zahara looked up from her laptop, her expression wary. "I don't know... I've never really done anything like that before."

"I get that," Nia said. "It can be intimidating. But it might be worth a try. They're there to help, and you don't have to do it alone. I can even go with you if you want."

Zahara hesitated, her fingers fidgeting with the edge of her blanket. "Maybe," she said finally. "I'll think about it."

"That's all I'm asking," Nia said with a smile. "Just think about it."

The next few days were a mix of small victories and lingering challenges. Zahara seemed to be making an effort to be more present, joining Nia for meals and even cracking jokes during their movie nights. But there were still moments when she withdrew, retreating into her thoughts or leaving the room without explanation. Nia tried to be patient, reminding herself that healing wasn't a linear process.

One evening, as they were sitting on Zahara's bed eating takeout, Zahara spoke up unexpectedly. "You've been really patient with me, Nia. I don't think I've ever had a friend like you before."

Nia looked at her, surprised. "What do you mean?"

"I mean... someone who doesn't give up on me," Zahara said. "I'm not used to that. It's scary, but it's also... nice."

Nia felt a lump form in her throat. "You're worth it, Zahara. You're an amazing person, even if you don't always see it."

Zahara smiled a genuine, unguarded smile that made Nia's heartache with a mix of sadness and hope. She knew Zahara's journey wasn't over, but in that moment, it felt like they were moving in the right direction—together.

Chapter 4
Cracks Beneath the Surface

The start of the week brought with it a fresh wave of busyness. Nia's calendar was rapidly filling up with deadlines, group project meetings, and study sessions. She tried to keep a positive outlook, convincing herself that staying busy would help her manage the growing stress of college life. But even as she juggled everything, Zahara remained in the back of her mind. Her friend had been more open lately, but Nia could tell there was still so much Zahara wasn't saying, and the weight of it all was clearly taking a toll.

Monday morning started with a psychology lecture that seemed to stretch on forever. Nia sat in the middle row, her laptop open, typing furiously as the professor rattled off complex diagrams and terms she could barely process. The material was overwhelming, and her confidence wavered as she glanced at the students around her—most of whom seemed to be keeping up without issue. She bit the inside of her cheek, forcing herself to focus. She didn't have time to dwell on self-doubt right now.

After class, Nia headed to the library to meet Leila and Chris for their group project. Leila greeted her with her usual energy, waving her arms as if Nia had been gone for weeks. "Nia! Thank goodness you're here. Chris has been grumbling about how we're behind schedule. You might want to help calm him down before he explodes."

Chris, seated across the table, rolled his eyes but didn't deny it. "We're not behind, but we're not ahead either," he muttered, tapping his pen against the table. "And with the professor's standards, we can't afford to be average."

"Good morning to you too, Chris," Nia said with a small laugh, setting her bag down. "Let's get to work then. No time to waste."

As the three of them worked, Nia felt the familiar pull of focus and productivity that came with tackling a shared goal. Leila's enthusiasm kept the mood light, while Chris's perfectionism pushed them to think critically about their approach. By the end of the session, they had a solid outline for their project, and Nia felt a flicker of pride. It was a small accomplishment, but in the chaos of college, even small wins felt significant.

Once their meeting ended, Nia checked her phone and saw a text from Zahara: *Want to grab dinner later? My treat.*

Nia smiled at the message. Zahara had been making an effort to spend more time with her lately, and it felt like progress. She quickly texted back: *Sounds good! Meet at the dining hall at 6?*

The hours flew by, and before Nia knew it, she was walking into the bustling dining hall. The smell of pizza and stir-fry filled the air, and the noise of students chatting and laughing echoed off the walls. She spotted Zahara at a corner table, scrolling through her phone. Her posture was relaxed, but there was a tension in her eyes that Nia had learned to notice.

"Hey," Nia said, sliding into the seat across from her. "What's good today?"

"Not much," Zahara said with a smirk. "But I figured you'd settle for the chicken tenders. They're the only halfway decent thing here."

Nia laughed, grateful for the familiar banter. They grabbed their food and settled back at the table, the conversation flowing easily. For a while, it felt like things were normal again—like they were just two friends enjoying a meal together. But as they finished eating, Zahara's smile faded, and her gaze drifted to the window.

"I'm thinking about going home this weekend," Zahara said suddenly, her voice quiet.

Nia blinked in surprise. "Home? For the whole weekend?"

Zahara nodded, her expression unreadable. "Yeah. My mom's been asking me to come back. She says she needs help sorting some things out with the divorce."

Nia hesitated, unsure of how to respond. She wanted to be supportive, but she also worried about how much Zahara was taking on. "Do you think that's a good idea? I mean, you've been under so much stress already."

Zahara sighed, running a hand through her hair. "I don't know, Nia. It's not like I have a choice. My mom depends on me, and if I don't help, everything will just fall apart."

Nia frowned. "That's a lot of responsibility to put on you. It's not fair."

"Fair or not, it's my reality," Zahara said, her tone sharper than usual. She immediately softened, shaking her head. "Sorry. I didn't mean to snap. I just... I don't know what else to do."

"It's okay," Nia said quickly. "I get it. I just want to make sure you're taking care of yourself too."

Zahara offered a small, weary smile. "Thanks, Nia. I'll be fine. I just need to get through this weekend."

Nia nodded, but a sense of unease settled in her chest. She didn't like the idea of Zahara going home to face more stress, especially when she was already stretched so thin. But she didn't want to push too hard and risk making things worse. Instead, she resolved to check in on Zahara throughout the weekend, even if it was just through text.

The rest of the week passed uneventfully, and by Friday afternoon, Zahara was packing a small duffel bag for her trip home. Nia watched from her desk, chewing on the end of her pen as she debated whether to say anything. Finally, she spoke up.

"Hey, Zahara?"

"Yeah?" Zahara glanced over, zipping up her bag.

"Just... don't forget that it's okay to set boundaries. You don't have to fix everything on your own."

Zahara's expression softened, and she gave Nia a grateful look. "I'll try. Thanks, Nia."

With that, Zahara slung her bag over her shoulder and headed out the door. Nia sat in the quiet dorm room, staring at the empty space where Zahara's bed was. She felt a pang of worry, but she pushed it aside, reminding herself that Zahara was strong and capable. Still, she couldn't shake the feeling that things were about to get more complicated.

That evening, Nia tried to distract herself by diving into her homework, but her thoughts kept drifting back to Zahara. She wondered how the weekend was going for her friend—whether she was managing okay or if things were harder than she'd anticipated. Nia considered texting her but decided to wait, not wanting to seem overbearing.

The next morning, Nia woke up to find a text from Zahara: *Made it home. It's... okay so far. I'll call you later.*

The message didn't do much to ease Nia's concerns, but she appreciated that Zahara had reached out. She spent the day running errands and meeting up with Leila to finalize their project presentation. Leila's chatter was a welcome distraction, and by the time Nia returned to her dorm, she felt slightly more at ease.

That night, as Nia was getting ready for bed, her phone buzzed with an incoming call. It was Zahara.

"Hey," Nia said, answering quickly. "How's it going?"

There was a long pause on the other end of the line before Zahara spoke. Her voice was strained, barely above a whisper. "Not great. My mom and dad were fighting all day. I tried to stay out of it, but they kept dragging me in. It's like... I don't even know how to describe it. Everything feels so broken."

Nia's heart ached at the raw pain in Zahara's voice. "I'm so sorry, Zahara. That sounds awful."

"It is," Zahara admitted. "And I just keep thinking... what if it's always going to be like this? What if I never get out of this mess?"

"You will," Nia said firmly. "This is just one part of your life, Zahara. It doesn't define your whole future."

Zahara didn't respond right away, but Nia could hear her breathing on the other end of the line. Finally, Zahara spoke, her voice trembling. "Thanks, Nia. I needed to hear that."

As the call ended, Nia sat in the dimly lit dorm room, her phone still clutched in her hand. She felt an overwhelming sense of helplessness, but also a fierce determination to be there for Zahara, no matter what. Whatever challenges lay ahead, she knew they would face them together.

The following day, Nia woke up to the gentle buzz of her alarm clock. The gray morning light spilled into the dorm room, painting everything in muted tones. Zahara hadn't called again, and though Nia told herself not to worry, the silence gnawed at her. She pulled out her phone, staring at the last text message Zahara had sent the day before.

Made it home. It's... okay so far. I'll call you later.

Nia debated whether to send a follow-up text, her thumb hovering over the keyboard. She didn't want to intrude or pressure Zahara into responding. But she couldn't just sit there doing nothing either. Finally, she typed out a quick message:

Hey, thinking of you. Hope today's better. Let me know if you need anything!

Hitting send, Nia tossed her phone onto her desk and tried to refocus on the long to-do list awaiting her. There was a stack of reading for communication, an essay draft that needed revising, and a club meeting she had reluctantly agreed to attend. But no matter how much she tried to immerse herself in work, her mind kept drifting back to Zahara.

At lunch, Nia sat alone in the dining hall, poking at a plate of spaghetti. The buzz of conversation around her felt distant as if she were trapped behind a glass wall. She hated this feeling of helplessness, this nagging sense that something was wrong but beyond her control.

"Hey, you good?" a familiar voice cut through her thoughts.

Nia glanced up to see Jordan standing across from her, a tray balanced in one hand and an inquisitive look on his face.

"Oh, hey," Nia said, mustering a small smile. "Yeah, I'm fine. Just tired, I guess."

Jordan set his tray down and slid into the seat across from her. "Tired or stressed? Because you look more stressed to me."

Nia shrugged. "Maybe both."

Jordan didn't push further, which Nia appreciated. Instead, he launched into a story about an awkward encounter he'd had in his chemistry lab that morning, complete with exaggerated impressions of his professor and classmates. Despite herself, Nia found herself laughing, the tension in her shoulders easing just a little.

"You're welcome," Jordan said with a playful smirk as Nia's laughter subsided.

"For what?"

"For cheering you up, obviously."

Nia rolled her eyes but couldn't suppress her grin. "Thanks, Jordan."

"Anytime," he said, leaning back in his chair. "But seriously, if you ever need to talk, I'm around. Don't let college stress eat you alive, okay?"

"I'll keep that in mind," Nia said, feeling a flicker of gratitude for his easygoing support.

The rest of the day passed in a blur of lectures and meetings, and by the time Nia returned to her dorm that evening, she was utterly drained. She kicked off her shoes and collapsed onto her bed, closing her eyes for what she intended to be a quick rest. But just as she was drifting off, her phone buzzed on the nightstand.

She sat up and grabbed it, her heart skipping a beat when she saw Zahara's name on the screen.

Hey, you free to talk?

Nia immediately dialed her friend's number, and Zahara picked up after the second ring.

"Hey," Zahara said, her voice sounding heavier than usual.

"Hey. I was just thinking about you," Nia said softly. "How are things?"

There was a long pause on the other end of the line, and Nia could hear Zahara exhale shakily. "Not great," Zahara admitted. "My parents... they've been fighting nonstop. And my mom keeps asking me to take sides like I'm supposed to choose between them."

Nia's chest tightened. "That's not fair to you, Zahara. You shouldn't have to be in the middle of all this."

"I know," Zahara said, her voice cracking. "But what am I supposed to do? If I don't help, it feels like I'm abandoning them. And if I do... it's like I'm losing myself in their mess."

"You're not abandoning them," Nia said firmly. "You're allowed to take care of yourself too. You can't pour from an empty cup, Zahara."

Zahara let out a bitter laugh. "Tell that to my mom. She keeps saying I'm the only one who can keep things together. It's like she doesn't even realize how much this is affecting me."

Nia wished she could reach through the phone and hug her friend. "I'm so sorry you're going through this," she said. "But you don't have to carry it all on your own. I'm here for you, okay? Whatever you need."

"Thanks, Nia," Zahara said, her voice softening. "That means a lot."

They talked for a while longer, Zahara opening up about the struggles she'd been keeping bottled up for so long. Nia listened intently, offering words of comfort where she could and simply being a sounding board when Zahara needed to vent. By the time they ended the call, Nia felt a mix of relief and sadness. She was glad Zahara had confided in her, but it was clear her friend was still carrying an immense burden.

That night, as Nia lay in bed staring at the ceiling, she couldn't shake the feeling that this was just the beginning of something bigger. Zahara's struggles were deeper than she'd realized, and Nia knew it would take more than a few supportive phone calls to help her friend through it.

The following morning, Nia woke up with a newfound sense of determination. If Zahara was going to fight through her challenges, then Nia would fight alongside her. She didn't know exactly how yet, but she was resolved to be the friend Zahara needed—even if it meant stepping out of her comfort zone.

After a quick breakfast, Nia decided to pay a visit to the campus counseling center. She wasn't sure what she was looking for—maybe advice on how to support Zahara, or even resources Zahara could use if she decided to seek help herself. The receptionist at the front desk greeted her warmly and handed her a brochure outlining the services available to students.

"Do you want to make an appointment?" the receptionist asked.

"Not right now," Nia said, tucking the brochure into her bag. "But thanks."

As she walked back to her dorm, Nia flipped through the brochure, her mind spinning with ideas. She couldn't force Zahara to seek professional help, but she could gently encourage her and let her know there were people who cared and wanted to help.

By the time Nia reached her dorm room, she felt a glimmer of hope. Maybe things weren't as hopeless as they seemed. Zahara was strong, and Nia had no doubt that, with the right support, her friend could overcome anything.

Later that evening, as Nia settled in to work on her psychology notes, her phone buzzed with another text from Zahara.

"Thanks for listening last night. I don't know what I'd do without you."

Nia smiled, her heart swelling with warmth.

"Anytime," she replied. "We'll get through this together."

As the days turned into weeks, Nia found herself becoming more attuned to Zahara's moods. She learned when to offer words of encouragement and when to simply sit in silence and let Zahara process her thoughts. Their friendship grew stronger in the process, and Nia began to realize that supporting someone else didn't mean she had to have all the answers. Sometimes, just being there was enough.

And though the road ahead was still uncertain, Nia felt more confident than ever that they could face it together.

The next few days passed in a haze of classes, late-night study sessions, and fleeting interactions between Nia and Zahara. While Zahara seemed slightly better after their heartfelt phone conversation, her usual spark still hadn't fully returned. Nia noticed how Zahara seemed to withdraw during their shared moments—she was quieter, distracted, and occasionally forced a smile that didn't quite reach her eyes. Nia wanted to help, but she wasn't sure how to approach the subject without making things worse.

It was a brisk Friday afternoon when Nia decided she needed to do something more tangible to cheer Zahara up. Zahara had always loved exploring new places, so Nia planned a small outing. She'd heard about a cozy café on the edge of campus that hosted open mic nights on Fridays, and she thought it might be the perfect low-pressure escape for both of them.

"Hey," Nia called out.

Zahara pulled out one earbud and looked up. "Oh, hey. What's up?"

"I was thinking," Nia began, trying to keep her tone casual, "we could go check out this café tonight. They're doing an open mic thing—poetry, music, that kind of stuff. It could be fun."

Zahara hesitated, her expression uncertain. "I don't know... I'm not really feeling up to crowds right now."

"It doesn't have to be a crowd," Nia said quickly. "We can just grab some coffee and hang out in the back. No pressure. I just thought it might be nice to get off campus for a bit."

Zahara looked torn, but after a moment, she sighed and nodded. "Okay. I guess it couldn't hurt."

Nia smiled, relieved. "Great. It'll be fun, I promise."

The café was smaller than Nia had imagined, with mismatched furniture and fairy lights strung along the walls. The warm, earthy smell of coffee filled the air, and the low hum of conversation blended with the strumming of a guitar as a student performed a soulful melody on the small stage. Nia led Zahara to a table near the back, far enough from the stage to avoid feeling like they were in the spotlight but close enough to enjoy the atmosphere.

"This is nice," Zahara admitted as she glanced around. "I like the vibe."

"Right? It's cozy," Nia said, scanning the menu.

They ordered drinks—Nia opting for a chai latte and Zahara choosing her go-to caramel macchiato—and settled into their seats. For the first time in what felt like weeks, Zahara's face softened, the tension in her shoulders easing as she took a sip of her drink.

"I used to go to places like this all the time back home," Zahara said, her voice tinged with nostalgia. "There was this one café that did live jazz nights. My mom and I would go together sometimes."

Nia perked up. "That sounds amazing. I didn't know you were into jazz."

Zahara smiled faintly. "Yeah, my mom's a big fan. She used to play it around the house all the time when I was a kid. I guess it kind of stuck."

Nia filed that detail away, happy to see Zahara opening up, even if just a little. The night unfolded gently, with the two of them chatting and laughing in between performances. A few students read heartfelt poetry, their words raw and honest, and one particularly talented guitarist brought the room to life with an original song that had everyone clapping along.

As the evening wound down, Nia noticed Zahara's posture had relaxed, her laughter coming more freely. It was a small victory, but Nia clung to it, hoping it was a step toward brighter days.

On their walk back to the dorm, Zahara suddenly turned to Nia, her expression earnest. "Thanks for dragging me out tonight. I didn't realize how much I needed this."

"I'm glad you came," Nia said sincerely. "You seemed like you were enjoying yourself."

"I was," Zahara admitted a hint of surprise in her voice. "It was nice to just... not think about everything for a while."

Nia hesitated for a moment before speaking again. "You know, if you ever want to talk about it—or not talk and just do stuff like this—I'm here. I mean it."

Zahara's eyes softened, and she nodded. "I know. And I appreciate it. More than I can say."

They walked the rest of the way in comfortable silence, the night air crisp but not biting. When they reached the dorm, Zahara gave Nia a quick hug before heading to her room. It was a small gesture, but it warmed Nia's heart.

The following week brought new challenges for both of them. Midterms loomed on the horizon, and the campus seemed to buzz with an undercurrent of stress. Nia found herself buried in communication notes and flashcards, her nights growing longer and her sleep shorter. Zahara, on the other hand, threw herself into her creative writing assignments, pouring her emotions into stories that Nia suspected were more personal than Zahara let on.

Despite their busy schedules, the two made an effort to carve out moments of reprieve—study breaks at the campus library, impromptu coffee runs, and late-night talks about anything and everything. Nia felt their bond strengthening with each passing day, and while she still worried about Zahara, she took comfort in the fact that her friend wasn't entirely shutting her out.

One evening, as they sat in the common room flipping through notes for an upcoming exam, Zahara suddenly spoke up. "You know, I've been thinking about going to the counseling center."

Nia looked up, her surprise quickly giving way to encouragement. "Really? That's amazing, Zahara. I think it could really help."

Zahara shrugged, fiddling with the edge of her notebook. "I don't know. It just feels... overwhelming, I guess. Like, where do I even start?"

"You don't have to have all the answers," Nia said gently. "That's what they're there for—to help you figure it out. And I can go with you if you want, at least for the first time."

Zahara glanced at her, a flicker of gratitude in her eyes. "Thanks, Nia. I'll think about it."

It wasn't a definitive answer, but it was a step in the right direction. Nia knew better than to push; Zahara needed to come to the decision on her own terms.

That night, as Nia lay in bed reflecting on their conversation, she felt a sense of hope she hadn't felt in weeks. Zahara was starting to open up, and while the road ahead might still be rocky,

Nia was determined to walk it with her friend every step of the way.

Little did Nia know, that the challenges they had faced so far were just the beginning. The weight of change was heavier than either of them had anticipated, but together, they were learning how to carry it.

As the semester continued, the pressure around campus intensified. The looming shadow of midterms seemed to stretch across every interaction, every late-night study session, and every class Nia attended. Yet, amid the chaos, her bond with Zahara became a source of stability—a grounding force that kept her from feeling completely swept away.

One crisp morning, Nia sat in her communication lecture, absently tapping her pen against her notebook. The professor's voice droned on about communication processes, but her thoughts were elsewhere. Zahara had seemed off again that morning. Despite her progress in opening up, there were still days when she retreated into herself, offering clipped responses and hollow smiles. Nia couldn't shake the feeling that something deeper was brewing beneath the surface, something Zahara wasn't ready to share.

When the lecture ended, Nia packed up her things and headed to the campus café where she and Zahara had planned to meet for lunch. The café was buzzing with students, the smell of freshly brewed coffee mingling with the chatter of conversations and the clatter of cups. Nia spotted Zahara near the window, staring out at the autumn leaves falling in lazy spirals.

"Hey," Nia greeted as she slid into the seat across from her. "How's your day going?"

Zahara blinked, as if pulled from a trance, and offered a small smile. "It's okay. Just... a lot on my mind, I guess."

Nia nodded, studying her friend's face. Zahara's usual vibrancy was dimmed, her eyes shadowed with a tiredness that went beyond physical exhaustion. "Do you want to talk about it?"

Zahara hesitated, her fingers tracing the rim of her coffee cup. "Not here," she said softly.

Nia leaned forward, lowering her voice. "Then let's go

somewhere else. We can walk, or—"

Zahara shook her head. "No, it's fine. I just... I'll tell you later. Let's eat."

Reluctantly, Nia let the subject drop. She didn't want to push Zahara too hard and risk making her retreat further. Instead, they talked about lighter topics—their classes, the upcoming student showcase, and a funny story Zahara told about one of her professors accidentally spilling coffee on his lecture notes. But even as they laughed, Nia could see the strain Zahara was trying to hide.

Later that evening, back in the dorm, Zahara knocked on Nia's door. Nia looked up from her desk, where she had been attempting to finish her psych readings, and immediately noticed the tension in Zahara's posture.

"Hey, come in," Nia said, closing her textbook and gesturing to the bed.

Zahara sat down, her movements slow and deliberate. She took a deep breath before speaking. "I think I'm ready to tell you what's been going on."

Nia's heart quickened. She nodded, keeping her expression calm. "I'm here. Whatever it is, I'm listening."

Zahara hesitated, her hands clasped tightly in her lap. "It's my family. Things back home aren't... great. My parents are going through a divorce and since I'm the only child I'm in the middle of everything, mediating and having to pick between parents is horrible. Every time I call home, my mom tries to act like everything's fine, but I can hear it in her voice. And my dad... he's been distant. Like, really distant. I don't know if it's the stress or something else, but it's like he's just... not there anymore."

Nia felt a pang of empathy as Zahara's voice wavered. "Zahara, I'm so sorry. That sounds incredibly hard."

"It is," Zahara admitted, her eyes glistening. "And I feel so helpless. I'm here, trying to focus on school, but I can't seem to get a break with them, keep putting me in the middle of everything. But what can I even do? I don't know what to do and it's stressing me out."

Nia reached out, placing a hand on Zahara's. "I'm so sorry to hear about your parents. You shouldn't feel stressed about what's going on and I'm sorry you're in the middle of everything. But just know you aren't doing anything wrong if you have to stand your ground and tell your parents that you don't need to be in the middle of what's going on between them. I'll always be here if you need me. I'm here to support you and help you just let me know."

Zahara nodded, though her expression remained heavy. "I know you're right. It's just... hard. And I hate feeling like I'm carrying this weight alone."

"You're not alone," Nia said firmly. "You have me, and I'm here for whatever you need. If you want to talk, vent, or just not think about it for a while, I've got you."

For the first time that night, a genuine smile broke through Zahara's sadness. "Thanks, Nia. That means a lot."

The days that followed felt lighter, at least for a time. Zahara seemed more at ease, her steps less weighed down by the burden she had been carrying. She even agreed to visit the campus counseling center, a decision Nia wholeheartedly supported. Though Zahara was nervous about the idea at first, her first session left her feeling cautiously optimistic.

"It wasn't as bad as I thought it would be," Zahara admitted as they walked back to their dorm afterward. "The counselor was really nice. She didn't push me to talk about anything I wasn't ready for."

"That's great," Nia said, smiling. "I'm proud of you for going. I know that wasn't easy."

Zahara shrugged, but there was a hint of pride in her expression. "It's a start, I guess."

Meanwhile, Nia faced her own challenges. Midterms were fast approaching, and she struggled to keep up with the demands of her classes. Late nights became her norm as she tried to absorb the endless stream of information from her textbooks and lecture notes. But despite the stress, she found herself leaning on Zahara just as much as Zahara leaned on her. Their friendship had become a mutual lifeline, a source of strength and comfort in an otherwise overwhelming world.

One night, as they sat in the common room studying, Zahara suddenly closed her laptop and looked at Nia. "You know, for all the chaos, I'm really glad we met."

Nia looked up, surprised by the sudden sentiment. "Me too. I don't know what I'd do without you."

Zahara smiled, a warmth in her eyes that made Nia's chest feel lighter. "We're going to get through this. All of it. Together."

Nia nodded, feeling a renewed sense of determination. Whatever challenges lay ahead—midterms, family struggles, or the ever-present uncertainty of the future—they would face them together. The weight of change might be heavy, but with Zahara by her side, Nia felt stronger than ever.

As the weeks progressed, the days seemed to blur together. Nia found herself getting into a rhythm with her studies, though the pressure of maintaining high grades still weighed heavily on her shoulders. She spent more and more time in the library, hunched over her communication textbooks and flashcards. At times, she felt like she was drowning in information—memories of high school feeling more distant as she struggled to find her footing in the fast-paced, competitive environment of college.

But amidst all the chaos, Nia couldn't help but notice that Zahara was still struggling. Though she had been making progress, there were still moments when she seemed distant or lost in thought. It was clear that her family situation was still weighing on her, and despite the strides she'd made in opening up, there were still days when she couldn't quite shake the anxiety that seemed to grip her.

One evening, as Nia finished another late-night study session in the common room, she spotted Zahara sitting in the corner by herself, her laptop open in front of her, but her attention was far from the screen. The room was quieter now, the usual buzz of students retreating into their respective study sessions as the night wore on. Zahara had her headphones in, but her body language was unmistakable—she was disconnected from whatever she was working on.

Nia gathered her things and walked over to Zahara's side.

"Hey," she said softly, nudging her friend's shoulder.

Zahara looked up, her face momentarily blank before she forced a smile. "Oh, hey. Sorry, I didn't see you there."

"You okay?" Nia asked, her voice laced with concern. "You've been kind of quiet tonight."

Zahara shrugged, adjusting her headphones. "I'm fine. Just... distracted, I guess. Lots of stuff on my mind."

Nia hesitated, unsure of whether she should push further. She didn't want to intrude on Zahara's space, but at the same time, she couldn't ignore the nagging feeling that something was wrong. "You know you can talk to me, right?"

Zahara's eyes flickered for a moment, and Nia saw the faintest trace of vulnerability. "I know. It's just... hard to talk about it sometimes."

Nia pulled up a chair and sat beside her. "I get it. But you don't have to do it alone. You never have to do it alone."

Zahara looked at her, her expression softening. "Thanks, Nia. I really appreciate it."

They sat in silence for a while, the low hum of the common room providing a comfortable background to their quiet companionship. Nia wasn't sure what Zahara needed in that moment—words of comfort, a distraction, or just the presence of someone who cared. But she was content to sit there with her, offering whatever support she could, knowing that sometimes the most meaningful thing you can do for someone is simply be there, without pressure or expectations.

Eventually, Zahara closed her laptop and turned to Nia, a small but sincere smile on her face. "I think I'm going to head to bed. Thanks for checking in on me. It's good to know I'm not the only one staying up late in this place."

Nia grinned. "I'm pretty sure I've become the queen of late-night study sessions. But seriously, if you ever want to talk more—or just get away from all the chaos—I'm always here."

"I know," Zahara said, her voice quiet but filled with warmth. "And I'm glad you are."

Nia sat there for a moment, thinking to herself, a mix of pride and concern swirling within her. Zahara was a fighter, Nia knew that much. She had seen it in the way Zahara handled her family struggles, the way she pushed forward even when everything felt like it was falling apart. But sometimes, even the strongest people needed someone to lean on.

The next few days were a blur of study sessions, last-minute cramming for midterms, and the constant hum of academic pressure. But even amidst the stress, Nia felt a growing sense of stability in her friendship with Zahara. The two of them had found a rhythm, supporting each other through the ups and downs of college life.

On the morning of their first midterm, Nia felt a wave of anxiety wash over her as she sat at her desk, reviewing her notes one last time. The exam was just around the corner, and the weight of it was enough to make her stomach churn. She glanced over at Zahara, who sat across the room, her expression focused and determined. Despite the chaos in her life, Zahara always seemed to find a way to push through.

"You ready for this?" Nia asked, trying to lighten the mood.

Zahara looked up from her notes and offered a tight-lipped smile. "As ready as I'll ever be. I've been cramming like a maniac all week."

Nia chuckled. "Same here. But we've got this. Just breathe."

They both stood up and gathered their things, making their way to the lecture hall where the midterm would take place. The room was already filling up with students, the air thick with nerves and anticipation. Nia's palms were sweaty as she took a seat, trying to calm her racing heart. She glanced at Zahara, who had already opened her test booklet, her face a picture of concentration.

The next hour felt like an eternity as Nia worked through the questions, each one more difficult than the last. Her mind seemed to be running in circles, but somehow, she powered through. When the final bell rang, signaling the end of the exam, Nia let out a breath she didn't realize she'd been holding. She looked over at Zahara, who was already gathering her things, her face calm but her eyes betraying a hint of exhaustion.

"How do you think you did?" Nia asked, offering a small smile.

Zahara shrugged, her eyes tired but resolute. "I think I did okay. But who knows? It's over now."

Nia nodded in agreement, the relief of the exam finally being behind them settling in. "Yeah, we'll see. But for now, let's go grab some lunch. I think we've earned it."

Zahara grinned. "Definitely. I'm starving."

As they made their way out of the lecture hall and into the bright afternoon, Nia felt a surge of gratitude. Midterms were tough, no doubt about it, but she and Zahara had made it through together. The weight of the challenges they faced was still heavy, but the two of them had found a way to share it—to help each other carry the load. And in that moment, Nia realized that, no matter what came next, they would always have each other to lean on.

Chapter 5
Cracks Beneath the Surface

The crisp fall air carried the faint scent of damp leaves as Nia made her way across campus. The golden glow of the late afternoon sun bathed everything in a warm light, but it did little to ease the tension she felt simmering inside. Midterms were over, but the sense of relief she'd expected hadn't arrived. Instead, there was a gnawing unease—a feeling that something was about to change, though she couldn't put her finger on what.

She clutched her bag tightly as she pushed through the doors of the student union, the familiar hum of chatter and the aroma of coffee greeting her. Zahara had texted her to meet there after class, but when Nia spotted her in their usual corner booth, she could tell right away that something was off. Zahara sat with her arms crossed, staring out the window, her lips pressed into a tight line.

"Hey," Nia said cautiously as she slid into the seat across from her. "What's up?"

Zahara barely glanced at her before returning her gaze to the window. "Nothing much," she said, her tone clipped.

Nia frowned, setting her bag down and leaning forward. "You sure? You seem... upset."

Zahara sighed, finally turning to face her. "It's just been one of those days," she admitted, her voice softer now but still tinged with frustration. "Classes are piling up, my mom's been texting me nonstop about things I can't help with, and to top it all off, I just got an email about a scholarship I didn't get. So, yeah. One of those days."

Nia reached across the table, her hand resting gently on Zahara's. "I'm sorry, Zahara. That really sucks. Is there anything I can do to help?"

Zahara shook her head, pulling her hand away and running it through her hair. "No, it's fine. I'll deal with it. I always do."

The words stung more than Nia expected, but she chose not to press. Instead, she offered a small, understanding smile. "Okay. But if you change your mind, you know I'm here."

Zahara nodded, her eyes softening for a moment before she changed the subject. "Anyway, how about you? How'd your midterms go?"

Nia hesitated, unsure if she should share her own struggles when Zahara was already dealing with so much. But she decided to be honest. "They were... rough. I think I did okay, but honestly, I'm just glad they're over."

Zahara gave a small laugh, the tension in her shoulders easing slightly. "Same. I feel like I've been running on fumes for weeks. Maybe we should treat ourselves—get some ice cream or something."

Nia's face lit up. "Now that's an idea I can get behind."

The two of them left the student union and headed to the campus ice cream shop, the cool breeze biting at their cheeks as they walked. For a little while, things felt normal again—like the weight of the world had been lifted, even if only temporarily. They laughed about the absurdity of their professors' expectations and swapped stories about their classmates. By the time they finished their cones, Zahara seemed more like herself, and Nia felt a renewed sense of hope that they could both handle whatever challenges came their way.

But the moment didn't last.

Later that night, back in their dorm, Nia was startled awake by the sound of Zahara's voice. It was muffled, but the urgency in her tone was unmistakable. She was on the phone again.

"I don't know what you want me to do!" Zahara hissed, her voice shaking. "I can't just drop everything and come home. I have my own stuff to deal with here."

Nia sat up in bed, her heart pounding. She didn't mean to eavesdrop, but the tension in Zahara's voice was impossible to ignore.

"I know things are hard right now," Zahara continued, her tone softening slightly. "But you can't continue to put me in the middle of everything. I'm doing the best I can, okay?"

There was a long pause, and then Zahara let out a frustrated sigh. "Fine. I'll figure something out. Just... don't call me in the middle of the night again. I need to sleep."

When Zahara ended the call, the room fell silent except for the sound of her shaky breathing. Nia debated whether to say something but ultimately decided against it. Zahara clearly needed space, and Nia didn't want to make things worse.

The next morning, Zahara was unusually quiet as they got ready for the day. Nia tried to act normal, but the tension between them was palpable. As they walked to class together, Zahara finally broke the silence.

"Sorry if I woke you up last night," she said, her voice low. "That was my mom. Once again I'm in the middle of everything."

"It's okay," Nia said quickly. "I didn't mean to overhear, but it sounded like you were upset. Are you sure you're okay?"

Zahara hesitated, her gaze fixed on the ground. "Honestly? No, I'm not. But I don't know what to do about it. My parents are making me choose sides and I don't know what to do, I'm barely keeping it together here as it is. I feel like I'm being pulled in a million directions, and I can't make anyone happy—not my parents, not my professors, not even myself."

Nia stopped walking, placing a hand on Zahara's arm to get her to look at her. "Zahara, you don't have to do this alone. You've been there for me so many times—let me be there for you now.

Whatever you need, I'm here."

Zahara's eyes filled with tears, and she quickly wiped them away. "Thanks, Nia. That means a lot. I just... I don't know how to fix this."

"You don't have to fix everything," Nia said gently. "Sometimes it's enough just to keep going. And you're not alone, okay? We'll figure this out together."

For the first time in days, Zahara smiled—a real, genuine smile. "You're the best, you know that?"

Nia grinned. "I try."

The rest of the day felt lighter somehow as if the weight Zahara had been carrying was slightly less oppressive now that she had shared it. Nia knew they still had a long way to go, but she was determined to help Zahara through it, no matter what it took.

That evening, as they sat studying together, Nia felt a sense of peace she hadn't felt in a long time. Despite the challenges they both faced, she knew they would get through it—together.

The week that followed brought a cautious sense of normalcy, though the air between Nia and Zahara still carried an unspoken tension. Zahara seemed lighter, as though some of the weight she carried had loosened its grip, but it wasn't completely gone. She wasn't entirely back to her old self, but there were moments when her laugh came easily, and her sharp wit sparkled in their conversations, making Nia hopeful that her friend was finding small spaces to breathe amidst the chaos.

Nia clung to those glimpses, even as she sensed there was still something Zahara wasn't sharing. One evening, as the dorm remained unusually quiet, they sat on the floor, books and notes sprawled out between them in preparation for a looming quiz.

Zahara tapped her pen rhythmically against her notebook, her brow furrowed in frustration as she stared at an intricate diagram of the digestive system. Nia sprawled out on her bed, looked up and could almost feel the invisible wall of tension Zahara had built around herself, radiating in waves across the room.

"Want to take a break?" Nia asked gently, setting her textbook aside and crossing her arms over her knees.

Zahara sighed heavily, tossing her pen onto her notebook with more force than necessary. "I think my brain officially hit maximum capacity like an hour ago," she said, leaning back against the wall with a groan.

Nia smiled, trying to lighten the mood. "Perfect timing, then. You know what that means? Snack time. I've got chips and cookies in the drawer, or—hear me out—we could take a late-night walk to the vending machines."

Zahara sat up slightly, considering the options, before pushing herself to her feet. "Vending machines. I need to move before I feel my legs permanently fusing into place."

As they stepped out into the crisp night air, Nia stretched her arms above her head and breathed deeply, savoring the stillness of the campus at this hour. The pathways glowed under the soft golden light of the lampposts, and the faint hum of crickets filled the silence. Zahara stuffed her hands into the pockets of her hoodie, her shoulders hunched slightly against the cool breeze.

"You know," Zahara said after a long moment of quiet, her voice carrying a pensive tone, "I used to love studying at night back in high school. The house would be quiet, everyone asleep, and it felt like I was the only person awake in the world. It was peaceful." She paused, kicking at a stray leaf on the ground. "I guess it's different now."

Nia glanced over at her, sensing the shift in Zahara's mood. "How's it different?" she asked, keeping her voice casual but curious.

Zahara shrugged, her gaze fixed on the path ahead. "Back then, the quiet felt comforting, you know? Like I could just focus on what needed to get done. Now it's just... heavy. Like the quiet is this reminder of everything I'm supposed to be doing but can't seem to figure out. It's like I'm running out of time, even when there's no one else around." Her voice softened toward the end, almost as if she regretted saying it aloud.

Nia frowned, her heart aching for her friend, but before she could respond, Zahara forced a small, wry smile. "Anyway, I'm probably just being dramatic. Let's get those snacks before I start waxing poetic about existential dread."

Nia laughed lightly, following Zahara's lead as they made their way to the vending machines. The familiar hum of the machines greeted them as they entered the student union, the fluorescent lights casting a faint glow over the empty space. Nia fumbled with the crumpled dollar bills she'd stuffed in her pocket, smoothing them out as she fed them into the machine.

Zahara stood beside her, scanning the options intently. "Skittles or chocolate?" Zahara asked, her finger hovering over the buttons.

"Chocolate. Obviously," Nia replied without hesitation, bending down to grab the bag of chips she had already selected. Zahara smirked, pressing the button for a candy bar. As it clattered down into the machine's slot, she picked it up and held it aloft triumphantly.

"Fuel for the sleep-deprived," she declared with a mock-serious tone that made Nia laugh.

They found a bench outside and sat down, the candy bar and chips balanced precariously between them. Nia tilted her head back to admire the night sky, the stars twinkling faintly against the inky darkness. The air was cool but refreshing, carrying with it the faint scent of grass and damp earth. "Do you ever think about where we'll be in five years?" Zahara asked suddenly, breaking the comfortable silence.

Nia tilted her head toward her friend, the question catching her off guard. "All the time," she admitted after a moment, her voice thoughtful. "But I try not to dwell on it too much. It's hard enough keeping up with the next five days, let alone five years."

Zahara chuckled softly, nodding in agreement. "Fair point," she said, unwrapping her candy bar and taking a bite. They fell into silence again, but it wasn't awkward or strained—it was the kind of silence that felt safe, where neither of them felt the need to fill the space with empty words. For a brief moment, everything felt simple, as though the weight of college, family, and the future could be paused, just for a little while.

The following weekend, Nia received a text from Jordan inviting her and Zahara to a small get-together at her apartment. Zahara hesitated at first, clearly torn between wanting a break from the dorm and not wanting to deal with too many people. But with some gentle encouragement from Nia, she eventually agreed.

Jordan's apartment was modest but inviting, the warm lighting and faint smell of buttered popcorn giving it a cozy, lived-in feel. A few other students were scattered around, chatting in small groups or lounging on the couch. Zahara hung back at first, but as the evening went on, she gradually began to relax. Nia watched as her friend drifted toward a group of students by the window, joining their conversation with ease. She couldn't help but feel a swell of pride as Zahara's natural charisma shone through, her laughter ringing out over the soft murmur of voices.

"You're lucky to have her," Jordan said, appearing beside Nia with a smile. "She seems like someone who's got a lot going on, but she handles it well. You both do."

Nia smiled, feeling a warmth spread through her chest. "Thanks," she said softly. "She's pretty great, isn't she?"

Jordan nodded, his expression turning thoughtful. "It's tough, balancing everything—college, life, all the expectations people have for you. But having someone in your corner makes all the difference."

Nia glanced over at Zahara again, who was laughing at something one of the students had said. "Yeah," she murmured, her voice barely audible. "It really does."

The night passed in a blur of laughter and music, and by the time Nia and Zahara left, the air between them felt lighter somehow. As they walked back to their dorm under the pale glow of the moon, Zahara admitted that she'd enjoyed herself more than she'd expected.

"Thanks for convincing me to go," she said, her tone uncharacteristically sincere. "I needed that."

Nia smiled, bumping Zahara's shoulder lightly. "Anytime," she replied. "That's what friends are for."

As the days passed, Nia found herself growing more attuned to the subtle shifts in Zahara's mood. Despite their shared moments of levity, there were still times when Zahara would retreat into herself, her gaze distant and her answers clipped. Nia didn't push—she had learned early on that Zahara wasn't the type to open up easily—but she made a point to be present, to let Zahara know she wasn't alone. It was during one of these quieter moments, a Sunday afternoon when the rain pattered softly against their dorm window, that Zahara finally spoke up. "Do you ever feel like... you're trying so hard to keep it all together, but no one really sees it?" she asked, her voice barely above a whisper.

Nia, who had been curled up with a book on her bed, looked up in surprise. She set the book aside and shifted to face Zahara, who was sitting cross-legged on her bed, staring at her laptop screen.

"Yeah," Nia said after a moment, her voice gentle. "I think everyone feels like that sometimes. Like no matter how much you do, it's never enough, and no one really notices how hard you're trying."

Zahara nodded slowly, her fingers tracing the edge of her laptop. "It's exhausting," she murmured, her voice tinged with a vulnerability that Nia hadn't heard before. "Sometimes I wonder if it's even worth it, you know? Like, what's the point of all this if I'm just going to keep feeling like I'm drowning?"

Nia's heart ached for her friend, and she leaned forward, resting her elbows on her knees. "I don't have all the answers," she admitted, her tone sincere. "But I do know that you don't have to figure it out alone. You've got me, Zahara. And I see how hard you're working, even if it feels like no one else does."

For a moment, Zahara didn't say anything, her gaze fixed on the rain streaking down the window. Then she let out a soft laugh, a sound that was equal parts relief and disbelief. "You're too good, you know that?" she said, glancing over at Nia with a small, grateful smile. "I don't know what I'd do without you." Nia smiled back, feeling a warmth spread through her chest. "Good thing you don't have to find out," she said lightly, earning a genuine laugh from Zahara.

The rest of the afternoon passed in companionable silence, the sound of rain creating a soothing backdrop as they worked on their respective assignments. Nia felt a sense of peace settle over her, a quiet reassurance that their friendship was becoming something steady and unshakable, a refuge in the often overwhelming world of college life.

Later that week, Zahara surprised Nia by suggesting they attend a campus workshop on mindfulness and stress management. "I figured it couldn't hurt," Zahara said with a shrug, her tone casual but her expression hopeful.

Nia agreed readily, eager to support her friend and curious about what the workshop would entail. When they arrived at the event, they were greeted by a small group of students sitting in a circle, the soft hum of calming music filling the room. The facilitator, a cheerful graduate student with a soothing voice, welcomed them warmly and introduced the evening's activities, which included guided meditation and journaling exercises.

At first, Nia felt a bit awkward, unsure of how to fully relax and let go of her thoughts. But as the facilitator led them through a series of breathing exercises, she found herself easing into the rhythm, her mind quieting in a way she hadn't experienced in a long time. Beside her, Zahara seemed equally at ease, her shoulders losing their usual tension as she closed her eyes and followed the instructions.

After the meditation, the group was given time to write in their journals, prompted by a series of reflective questions about stress, resilience, and self-care. Nia found herself writing freely, her thoughts spilling onto the page as she explored her own struggles and triumphs over the past few weeks. When the session ended, she felt lighter, as though she had unpacked a suitcase she hadn't even realized she'd been carrying.

Walking back to their dorm, Zahara turned to Nia with a thoughtful expression. "That was... surprisingly helpful," she admitted, her tone almost reluctant. "I didn't think I'd actually get anything out of it, but I feel like I can breathe a little easier now." Nia smiled, her own heart feeling lighter as well.

"Yeah, me too," she said. "Maybe we should make this a regular thing."

Zahara nodded, a small but genuine smile tugging at her lips. "Yeah," she said softly. "I think I'd like that."

As the semester continued, Nia and Zahara found themselves settling into a rhythm, their friendship growing stronger with each passing day. They tackled their classes together, shared late-night study sessions fueled by caffeine and laughter, and leaned on each other during moments of doubt and stress. But beneath the surface, Nia couldn't shake the feeling that there was still something Zahara wasn't telling her, a shadow that lingered even in their brightest moments.

That shadow became harder to ignore one evening when Nia returned to their dorm after a long day of classes and found Zahara sitting on the edge of her bed, her phone clutched tightly in her hand. Her expression was a mix of frustration and sadness, her brows knit together as she stared down at the screen.

"Hey," Nia said cautiously, setting her backpack down by her desk. "Everything okay?"

Zahara looked up, her eyes briefly meeting Nia's before she looked away, her jaw tightening. "It's nothing," she said quickly, her tone clipped.

Nia hesitated, unsure of whether to push for more information or give Zahara the space she seemed to need. "If you want to talk about it, I'm here," she said gently, sitting down on her own bed and folding her hands in her lap.

Zahara let out a heavy sigh, her shoulders slumping as she set her phone aside. "It's just... complicated," she said after a moment, her voice tinged with exhaustion. "My family doesn't really get what it's like to be here, to be doing this. They think I'm just living the dream, but they don't see how hard it is. And when I try to explain, it's like they don't want to hear it."

Nia nodded, her heart aching for her friend. "That sounds really hard," she said softly. "I can't imagine how frustrating that must be, feeling like you're not being heard."

Zahara gave a small, bitter laugh, running a hand through her hair. "Yeah, well, it's nothing new," she said. "I've always been the one who's supposed to have it all together, you know? The responsible one, the one who makes everyone else proud. But sometimes I just want to scream and tell them that I'm not perfect, that I'm struggling too."

Nia reached out, placing a hand on Zahara's arm. "You don't have to be perfect," she said firmly. "Not for them, not for anyone. You're doing your best, and that's enough. And if they can't see that right now, it doesn't mean they never will."

Zahara looked at Nia, her eyes glistening with unshed tears, and for a moment, Nia thought she might cry. But instead, Zahara smiled—a small, fragile smile, but a smile nonetheless. "Thanks, Nia," she said quietly. "You're a good friend."

Over the next few weeks, the strain between Zahara and her family seemed to settle into the background, but Nia could tell it hadn't disappeared entirely. Zahara had always been good at putting up walls, smiling her way through tough days and acting as if nothing fazed her. But Nia had come to know her well enough to recognize the cracks beneath the surface—the way her laughter didn't quite reach her eyes, the way she distracted herself by diving headfirst into assignments and social events.

Nia wanted to help, but she also didn't want to push Zahara too hard. Instead, she focused on being a steady presence, someone Zahara could lean on when she was ready. Meanwhile, Nia found herself grappling with her own challenges. Her psychology class was proving to be far more difficult than she had anticipated, and no matter how many hours she spent poring over her notes and textbook, the concepts refused to stick.

After a particularly grueling quiz, Nia slumped into a chair in the library, dropping her head onto the table with a groan. She was supposed to meet Zahara for their usual study session, but at this point, she wasn't sure if she had the energy to even open her notebook.

"Rough day?" a familiar voice asked.

Nia lifted her head to see Jordan standing across from her, a concerned look on his face. He held a coffee cup in each hand and set one down in front of her. "Figured you could use this," he said with a small smile.

"Thanks," Nia mumbled, wrapping her hands around the warm cup. "I don't know if coffee is enough to save me, though. I think I bombed my quiz."

Jordan pulled out a chair and sat down across from her. "That bad, huh?"

Nia nodded, taking a sip of the coffee. It was just the right amount of bitterness, and she felt a small flicker of gratitude for Jordan's thoughtfulness. "I don't know what I'm doing wrong," she admitted. "I study, I go to class, I ask questions, but it's like none of it sticks. I'm starting to wonder if I'm even cut out for this."

Jordan leaned back in his chair, studying her for a moment. "You ever think maybe you're being too hard on yourself?" he asked. "College isn't easy. No one gets it right all the time."

"Yeah, but it feels like everyone else is managing just fine," Nia said, her frustration bubbling to the surface. "Zahara's acing her classes, my group members always seem so confident, and then there's me—barely scraping by."

Jordan frowned. "You don't know that," he said gently. "People are really good at hiding when they're struggling. I bet Zahara has her own stuff she's dealing with, even if she doesn't show it."

Nia hesitated, thinking about Zahara's guarded demeanor and the tension she'd seen in her friend's eyes. "Maybe," she admitted. "But that doesn't change the fact that I feel like I'm drowning."

Jordan leaned forward, his expression earnest. "Then let people help you," he said. "Talk to your professor, join a study group, ask Zahara for help. You don't have to do this alone, Nia."

His words struck a chord, and Nia found herself nodding slowly. "You're right," she said, though the thought of asking for help still made her stomach twist with anxiety. "I'll figure something out."

"Good," Jordan said with a grin. "Because I'm not letting you give up that easily. You've got too much potential for that."

Before Nia could respond, Zahara appeared at the edge of the table, her backpack slung over one shoulder. "Hey," she said, her eyes darting between Nia and Jordan. "What's going on?"

"Just a little pep talk," Jordan said, standing up and grabbing his coffee. "I'll leave you two to it. See you around, Nia."

Nia watched him go, her heart feeling a little lighter despite her earlier frustration. Zahara slid into the seat he had vacated, raising an eyebrow. "You and Jordan seem to be getting close," she said, her tone teasing.

Nia rolled her eyes. "It's not like that," she said, though she couldn't deny that she appreciated Jordan's support. "He's just a friend."

"Uh-huh," Zahara said, smirking. "Whatever you say."

The teasing eased some of the tension that had been hanging over Nia, and she smiled despite herself. "How was your day?" she asked, changing the subject.

Zahara sighed, pulling out her laptop and setting it on the table. "Long," she said. "But I got through it. You?"

"Same," Nia said. "I think I bombed my psychology quiz."

Zahara winced in sympathy. "Oof. That sucks. Do you want to go over the material together? Maybe we can figure out what went wrong."

Nia hesitated, remembering Jordan's advice. She hated feeling like a burden, but Zahara's offer felt genuine, and she knew she needed help. "Yeah," she said finally. "I'd really appreciate that."

The two of them spent the next hour reviewing Nia's notes and going over practice problems. Zahara was patient and encouraging, breaking down the concepts in a way that finally started to make sense. By the time they packed up their things and headed back to their dorm, Nia felt a flicker of hope that she could turn things around.

As they walked across campus, the cool evening air brushing against their faces, Zahara turned to Nia with a thoughtful expression. "You know," she said, "you don't give yourself enough credit. You're smarter than you think, Nia. You just need to believe it."

Nia smiled, her chest swelling with gratitude for her friend. "Thanks, Zahara," she said softly. "That means a lot."

When they reached their dorm, Zahara hesitated at the door, her hand hovering over the handle. "Listen," she said, her voice quieter now. "I know I've been... off lately. And I just want you to know that it's not about you. I've just got some stuff I'm trying to work through."

Nia nodded, her heart aching for Zahara. "I'm here if you ever want to talk about it," she said.

Zahara gave her a small, grateful smile. "I know," she said. "Thanks, Nia."

The words warmed Nia's heart, and she followed Zahara inside, feeling a renewed sense of determination. They were both struggling in their own ways, but they had each other—and for now, that was enough.

Later that evening, as Nia sat on her bed scrolling mindlessly through her phone, Zahara emerged from her side of the room, wrapped in her favorite oversized hoodie. She had a distant look in her eyes, one that Nia was beginning to recognize as her retreating into her own world. Zahara leaned against the desk, toying absentmindedly with the drawstring of her hoodie.

"You okay?" Nia asked, setting her phone down. She didn't want to pry, but the silence between them felt heavier than usual.

Zahara blinked as if snapping out of a daze and gave a half-smile. "Yeah, just tired," she said, though her tone betrayed her words.

"You sure?" Nia pressed gently. "Because if something's on your mind, you can talk to me. I'm serious, Zahara. I know I haven't known you for that long, but I care about you. You don't have to go through everything alone."

Zahara hesitated, her fingers still tugging at the hoodie's drawstring. For a moment, Nia thought she might brush her off again, but then Zahara sighed and crossed the room, sitting on the edge of Nia's bed.

"It's just..." Zahara began, her voice soft. "Sometimes I feel like I'm carrying so much, you know? With school, with my family... it's like I'm always trying to keep it together because if I don't, everything will fall apart."

Nia nodded, staying quiet to give Zahara space to keep going.

"I try to help as much as I can, but it's hard being so far away. My mom is stressed to her breaking point. She called me earlier, saying she can't afford to go through with the divorce, and I feel so helpless because I can't help her, and I'm tired of being in the middle."

Nia's heart ached as she listened. She reached out and placed a hand on Zahara's arm, squeezing gently. "I'm so sorry, Zahara," she said. "That sounds like so much to deal with."

"It is," Zahara admitted, her voice cracking. "And the worst part is, I feel guilty for even being here. Like, I'm chasing my dreams while my family is struggling back home. Sometimes I wonder if I should just drop out and go back to help them."

"No," Nia said firmly, shaking her head. "Zahara, you can't do that. You're working so hard, and you deserve to be here. I know it's tough, but being here doesn't mean you don't care about your family. If anything, it shows how much you do care. You're building a future for yourself—and for them."

Zahara wiped at her eyes, a small, watery smile breaking through. "You're too good, Nia," she said. "I don't know what I'd do without you."

"Good thing you don't have to find out," Nia said, grinning. "We're in this together, okay? If you ever feel like it's too much, just tell me, and we'll figure it out. Promise me you'll talk to me next time you're feeling like this."

Zahara nodded, her smile growing a little steadier. "I promise," she said.

The moment felt like a turning point, a deepening of their friendship that Nia hadn't realized she needed so badly. She had spent so much time worrying about whether she belonged in college, whether she was good enough, that she hadn't stopped to appreciate the connections she was building. Zahara wasn't just her roommate or her study partner—she was becoming one of Nia's closest friends.

The next morning, Nia woke up feeling a strange mix of exhaustion and determination. Her psychology class was still looming over her like a dark cloud, but she resolved to take Jordan's advice and ask for help. After their lecture, she approached her professor, a kind but no-nonsense woman named Dr. Patel, who was gathering her things at the front of the classroom.

"Excuse me, Dr. Patel," Nia said, her voice wavering slightly. "Do you have a moment? I wanted to ask about the quiz we had last week. I... didn't do so well, and I was hoping you could help me figure out what I'm doing wrong."

Dr. Patel looked up, her expression softening. "Of course, Nia," she said. "I'm glad you came to talk to me. Let's sit down and go over it together."

As they reviewed the quiz, Nia felt a glimmer of hope. Dr. Patel explained the concepts patiently, pointing out where Nia had misunderstood and offering tips for how to approach similar problems in the future. By the time their meeting ended, Nia felt like she had a clearer path forward.

"Thank you so much," she said as she gathered her things. "I really appreciate it."

"Don't hesitate to reach out if you need more help," Dr. Patel said with a warm smile. "You're capable, Nia. You just need to trust yourself."

Buoyed by the professor's encouragement, Nia threw herself into her studies with renewed vigor. She joined a study group, started attending office hours regularly, and made a schedule to keep herself on track. It wasn't easy, and there were still moments of doubt, but she began to see small improvements.

Meanwhile, Zahara seemed lighter after their heart-to-heart. She still had her moments of stress, but she was more open about them now, and Nia made a point to check in with her regularly. They fell into a routine of supporting each other, sharing their highs and lows, and leaning on one another when things got tough.

One evening, as they sat on the floor of their dorm eating takeout and listening to music, Zahara turned to Nia with a curious expression.

"Have you thought about what you want to do after college?" she asked.

Nia paused, caught off guard by the question. "Not really," she admitted. "I guess I've just been so focused on getting through each day that I haven't thought that far ahead."

Zahara nodded thoughtfully. "Me neither," she said. "But I think about it sometimes. Like, what kind of life I want to build for myself. It's scary, but it's also kind of exciting, you know?"

Nia smiled. "Yeah," she said. "It is. I just hope we figure it out along the way."

Zahara grinned, raising her takeout container like a toast. "Here's to figuring it out," she said.

Nia laughed, clinking her own container against Zahara's. At that moment, with the music playing softly in the background and the warmth of their friendship wrapping around her like a blanket, Nia felt something she hadn't felt in a long time: hope.

They still had a long road ahead of them, full of challenges and uncertainties, but for the first time, Nia believed they could face it—together.

Chapter 6
Balancing Acts

The crisp night breeze carried a faint chill as Nia walked across campus the next morning, clutching her thermos of coffee and still shaken from oversleeping and rushing to make it to her first class. Zahara had already left for her early lecture, leaving Nia to navigate the day alone, her mind buzzing with memories of their quiet stargazing the night before—a rare moment of calm amidst her increasingly chaotic schedule.

It had been comforting, the way Zahara seemed to always know what to say to ease Nia's worries, but now, in the harsh light of day, reality weighed heavy on her shoulders again. As she rounded the corner near the student union, she spotted Jordan leaning casually against a lamppost, chatting with a group of friends. His presence was as familiar as ever, but something in his posture felt different—stiffer, maybe a little guarded.

When he saw her, his easygoing smile faltered briefly before he waved her over, a gesture that left her with little choice but to approach despite the hesitation gnawing at her. Reluctantly, she adjusted her bag and walked toward him, already anticipating the awkwardness that seemed to be brewing between them.

"Hey, stranger," Jordan greeted his tone light but carrying an edge that Nia couldn't quite place. "You've been busy avoiding me or what?"

Nia forced a laugh, though her mind still buzzed with the endless to-do list that awaited her. "Not avoiding you," she said, trying to keep her tone breezy. "Just drowning in work, you know how it is."

Jordan tilted his head, his smile fading just a bit. "Right," he said, his arms crossing in front of him. "Well, glad I caught you. Are we still on for study group tomorrow?"

Nia hesitated, her mind scrambling as she realized she had completely forgotten about their plan. Between juggling assignments and leaning on Zahara for help in psych class, the study group had slipped her mind entirely. "Uh... tomorrow might be tricky," she admitted, her voice faltering. "I've got an essay due, and, um, Zahara and I were going to go over some notes for class."

Jordan raised an eyebrow, his expression unreadable but tense. "Zahara, huh?" he said, his voice laced with something that sounded suspiciously like irritation.

"Yeah," Nia said cautiously, unsure of where this was going. "She's been helping me stay on top of things. It's been a crazy week."

Jordan let out a soft chuckle, though it lacked any real humor. "Seems like you two have been spending a lot of time together lately," he said, his tone light but his words pointed. "Guess I've been bumped down the priority list."

Nia blinked, taken aback by the sudden shift in his demeanor. "What? No, that's not—Jordan, it's not like that," she said quickly, her voice rising slightly as she tried to explain. "I've just been trying to balance everything. It's not about—"

"Hey, no need to explain," Jordan interrupted, holding up his hands in mock surrender. "I get it. You've got a lot going on. I just thought I don't know... Maybe we were close enough that you'd still make time for me. But whatever."

Nia's stomach twisted painfully at his words, guilt flooding her even as a flicker of defensiveness rose in her chest. This wasn't like him—Jordan had always been her rock, the one person she could rely on to be steady and supportive. But now, he seemed distant, almost accusatory, and she didn't know how to bridge the gap that had suddenly opened between them.

"Jordan," she began softly, taking a step closer. "I'm not trying to push you away. I—"

"Forget it," he said, cutting her off again with a shake of his head. He glanced over his shoulder at his friends, who were beginning to glance their way, clearly curious about the tension. "I'll see you around, Nia."

Before she could say anything else, Jordan turned and walked back to his group, leaving her standing there in the middle of the crowded pathway, a storm of emotions swirling inside her. She wanted to chase after him, to make him understand that she hadn't meant to hurt him, but her feet felt rooted to the ground. The weight of his words hung heavy in the air, and for the rest of the day, they replayed in her mind on an endless loop, fueling a growing sense of guilt and frustration. *Had she really been neglecting him?* She didn't think so—she had been doing her best to juggle everything. But maybe he had a point.

Back at the dorm later that evening, Zahara noticed Nia's mood almost immediately.

"You good?" Zahara asked as she sat on her bed, pulling out her laptop and glancing at Nia with concern.

Nia sighed heavily, setting her bag down and flopping onto her own bed. "Jordan's mad at me," she admitted, her voice tinged with exhaustion.

Zahara raised an eyebrow, leaning back against her pillows. "Mad? About what?"

"I don't know," Nia said, running a hand through her hair in frustration. "He thinks I've been spending too much time with you or something. He said I'm not making time for him."

Zahara smirked slightly, though her tone remained thoughtful. "Jealousy, huh? That's interesting."

"It's not like that," Nia said quickly, though her cheeks flushed at the implication. "He's just... I don't know. I think he's feeling left out or something."

Zahara's expression softened, her gaze steady as she studied Nia. "Sounds like his problem, not yours," she said simply. "You're not responsible for his feelings, Nia. If he can't handle you having other friends, that's on him."

Nia frowned, unsure how to respond. Zahara's bluntness was refreshing, but it didn't make the knot in her chest loosen. "It's not that simple," she said after a moment. "Jordan has always been there for me. I don't want to lose that."

Zahara nodded slowly, her tone softening further. "I get that," she said. "But you've got to set boundaries, you know? You can't let him make you feel guilty for living your life."

Nia nodded again, though her mind still churned with uncertainty. She wanted to believe Zahara was right, but a part of her couldn't help but feel responsible for the tension between her and Jordan. Later, as she worked on her lab report, her phone buzzed with a text from Zahara, inviting her to an open mic night at the student union. Grateful for the distraction, Nia agreed, and the two of them headed out, the lively atmosphere and soothing music briefly lifting Nia's spirits—until she spotted Jordan sitting across the room with another girl, laughing and chatting as if nothing had happened.

Nia's gaze lingered on Jordan from across the room, the laughter he shared with the unfamiliar girl sending a strange pang through her chest. She hated how much it affected her, hated how she couldn't look away even though every second she spent watching made her feel worse. Zahara, who had been rattling off playful commentary about the performers on stage, noticed the shift in Nia's demeanor and followed her line of sight. When she saw Jordan, Zahara's lips pressed into a thin line.

"Let me guess," Zahara said, leaning closer so her voice wouldn't carry over the crowd. "That's him?"

Nia nodded reluctantly, tearing her gaze away and focusing on the performer strumming a guitar on stage. "Yeah. That's him," she muttered.

Zahara tilted her head, studying Jordan from afar before glancing back at Nia. "You're really letting him get in your head, aren't you?"

"It's not that," Nia said quickly, though the heat rising to her cheeks betrayed her. "I just... I don't know. I feel bad about how things ended earlier. And now it looks like he's totally fine like it didn't even bother him."

Zahara snorted softly. "Trust me, he's not fine. Guys like him are never fine—they just pretend they are to make you feel worse. Classic manipulation tactic."

"It's not like that," Nia said, though even as the words left her mouth, she wasn't sure she believed them. "Jordan's not like that. He's a good guy."

"I'm sure he is," Zahara said, her tone even. "But good guys can still have a hard time letting go of control. Just saying."

Nia didn't respond, instead forcing herself to focus on the stage. She wanted to push Zahara's words aside, but they lingered in her mind, poking at her insecurities and making her wonder if there was some truth to them. As the night wore on, Zahara did her best to keep Nia distracted, cracking jokes and encouraging her to clap along with the performances. Nia appreciated the effort, even though her heart wasn't fully in it.

When the event ended, Zahara suggested grabbing milkshakes at the diner down the street, a last-ditch effort to salvage Nia's mood. As they walked through the crisp night air, Nia couldn't help but bring up the subject again.

"Do you think I'm a bad friend?" she asked, her voice tentative.

Zahara stopped mid-step, turning to face her. "What? No, of course not. Why would you even ask that?"

Nia hesitated, wrapping her arms around herself as they walked. "I don't know. It's just... Jordan made me feel like I haven't been there for him like I've been prioritizing other things over our friendship. And maybe he's right. Maybe I have been."

Zahara sighed, her breath visible in the cold air. "Nia, listen to me. You're not a bad friend. You're just one person trying to juggle a million things at once. If Jordan can't understand that, then that's on him, not you. You don't owe him every second of your time."

Nia nodded, though the guilt still lingered. She wanted to

believe Zahara, but a part of her couldn't help but still feel responsible for the growing distance between her and Jordan.

When they reached the diner, Zahara ordered a strawberry milkshake while Nia opted for chocolate. The bright neon lights and the smell of sizzling burgers provided a comforting contrast to the chilly night outside, and for a while, the tension in Nia's chest eased as they chatted about lighter topics. But just as their shakes arrived, the diner door swung open, and in walked Jordan, accompanied by the same girl from the open mic night.

Nia froze, her hand gripping her straw as she tried to blend into the background. Zahara noticed immediately and followed her gaze, her expression hardening when she spotted Jordan.

"Great timing," Zahara muttered under her breath.

Jordan didn't notice them at first, too engrossed in conversation with the girl, who was laughing at something he said. But as they moved to a booth near the back, his eyes landed on Nia. For a brief moment, his expression faltered, and something unreadable passed across his face. Nia quickly looked away, focusing on her milkshake as if it were the most fascinating thing in the world.

"You want to leave?" Zahara asked quietly, leaning closer.

"No," Nia said quickly, though her voice wavered. "I'm fine. It's fine."

Zahara didn't look convinced, but she didn't press the issue. Instead, she launched into a story about her childhood, her voice loud and animated, clearly an attempt to distract Nia from Jordan's presence. It worked for a while—Nia even managed to laugh at a particularly ridiculous anecdote about Zahara accidentally setting her science project on fire in eighth grade.

But her laughter died when she saw Jordan heading toward their table.

"Hey," he said, stopping beside them and shoving his hands into his pockets.

Nia looked up, her stomach twisting at the awkwardness of the situation.

"Hey," she replied, her voice soft.

Zahara raised an eyebrow but didn't say anything, sipping her milkshake as she watched the interaction unfold.

"Can we talk?" Jordan asked, his gaze flickering between Nia and Zahara. "Alone?"

Nia hesitated, glancing at Zahara, who gave her a small nod.

"Go ahead," Zahara said, though her tone carried a subtle warning.

Reluctantly, Nia stood and followed Jordan to a quieter corner of the diner. He didn't speak right away, instead running a hand through his hair as if trying to find the right words.

"Look," he said finally, his voice low. "I'm sorry if I came off as a jerk earlier. I just... I don't know. I feel like I'm losing you, Nia. Like we're not as close as we used to be."

Nia's heart ached at his words, but she forced herself to stay calm. "Jordan, I'm not trying to push you away," she said gently. "I've just been busy, and things have been overwhelming. It's not about you."

"I get that," Jordan said, though his tone suggested otherwise. "But it feels like you don't need me anymore. Like you've replaced me with Zahara."

"That's not true," Nia said quickly, her voice firm. "Zahara's been helping me, yes, but that doesn't mean you're any less important to me. I just... I need you to understand that I can't always be everything to everyone."

Jordan sighed, looking down at the floor. "I just miss how things used to be," he admitted.

Nia nodded, her chest tightening. "I miss it too, and we will get back to how things were I promise," she said softly.

Jordan didn't reply right away, and for a moment, they stood in silence, the hum of the diner filling the space between them. Finally, he nodded. "Okay," he said. "I'll put forth effort to make sure everything goes back to normal. But just... don't forget about me, okay?"

"I won't," Nia promised, though she wasn't sure if it was a promise she could keep.

As they returned to their respective tables, Nia couldn't shake the feeling that their friendship had shifted in a way that couldn't be undone. Zahara gave her a questioning look, but Nia just shook her head, signaling that she didn't want to talk about it.

The walk back to the dorm was steeped in silence, the cool night air pressing around Nia and Zahara as they passed under the flickering streetlights, their shadows stretching long across the pavement.

Nia pulled her jacket tighter around her body, her thoughts circling the unresolved tension with Jordan like vultures over a carcass. His words from the diner echoed relentlessly in her head—how he felt replaced, how he missed the simplicity of their bond. Nia tried to tell herself that she was just managing the best she could and that she didn't mean to push Jordan away.

Zahara seemed to sense the turbulence brewing in her friend, but she didn't push. When they finally reached the dorm, Zahara hesitated, glancing at Nia as she unlocked the door. "You okay?" she asked gently, stepping inside and dropping her bag onto her desk.

Nia hesitated, torn between brushing it off and confessing the storm raging inside her. "Yeah," she finally said, her voice flat as she sank onto her bed and stared at the ceiling. "It's just... complicated."

Zahara sat down across from her, tilting her head in a way that said she was analyzing everything without prying too much. "Look," Zahara said carefully, "I don't know Jordan that well, but I do know this: you're allowed to grow. You're allowed to change. If he can't handle that, it's on him, not you."

Nia nodded the truth of Zahara's words settling uncomfortably in her chest. "I know," she murmured, though her voice lacked conviction. "It's just hard. He's been there for me. I don't want to lose that."

Zahara leaned forward, her expression softening. "Then don't," she said simply. "But don't lose yourself trying to keep him happy, either."

The conversation lingered with Nia as she prepared for bed, Zahara's words echoing alongside Jordan's. She tried to push everything aside, focusing instead on the mundane act of brushing her teeth and organizing her books for the next day, but the unresolved feelings clawed their way to the surface, following her even as she slipped under the covers and turned out the lights. Sleep came reluctantly, haunted by fragmented dreams of childhood memories and an ever-growing distance between her and Jordan.

The next day, Nia threw herself into her classes with a ferocity that bordered on desperation. She took meticulous notes, asked questions during lectures, and even stayed after class to clarify points with her professors. But no matter how much she tried to immerse herself in academics, her mind kept drifting back to Jordan, replaying their conversation in the diner like a broken record. By the time her last class ended, she felt emotionally drained, her energy spent on suppressing the thoughts she couldn't escape.

As she packed up her things, her phone buzzed with a text from Zahara: *Study session in the library. You in?*

Nia stared at the message for a moment, debating whether she had the mental bandwidth for social interaction. After a long pause, she typed back: *Be there in 10.*

The library was a hive of activity, the faint hum of whispered conversations blending with the rustle of pages and the tapping of laptop keys. Nia spotted Zahara near the back, seated at a table with her laptop open and a coffee cup steaming beside her. "Hey," Nia said as she approached, dropping her bag onto the floor and collapsing into the chair opposite Zahara.

Hey," Zahara replied, sliding a second coffee cup across the table. "Figured you might need this."

Nia smiled, touched by the gesture. "You're a lifesaver," she said, taking a grateful sip. They worked in companionable silence for the next hour, occasionally exchanging notes or suggestions. For the first time all day, Nia felt a semblance of calm, the weight of her worries momentarily lifting as she focused on her assignments. But just as she was beginning to relax, her phone buzzed with another message.

Jordan: *Can we talk? I feel like we left things unfinished.*

Nia's heart sank as she read the message. She wanted to ignore it, to pretend she hadn't seen it, but she knew she couldn't avoid Jordan forever. With a sigh, she typed out a quick response: *Not right now. Maybe later.*

Zahara noticed the shift in Nia's expression and looked up from her laptop. "What's up?" she asked, her brow furrowing in concern.

"Jordan," Nia admitted, setting her phone face down on the table. "He wants to talk again." Zahara frowned, leaning back in her chair. "Didn't you just talk to him last night?"

Nia nodded, her frustration bubbling to the surface. "Yeah, but I guess it wasn't enough. I don't know what else to say to him."

Zahara shrugged, her tone pragmatic. "Maybe you don't have to say anything. Maybe it's time he figures things out on his own."

Nia nodded, though she wasn't sure if she agreed. Part of her wanted to reach out, to fix things, but another part of her was exhausted by the constant effort it took to keep their friendship intact. The evening dragged on, the words in her textbooks blurring together as her thoughts kept drifting back to Jordan. She couldn't shake the feeling that their relationship was reaching a breaking point, one that she wasn't sure they could come back from.

Later that night, back in the dorm, Nia found herself scrolling through old photos of her and Jordan on her phone. Each image brought back memories of simpler times—late-night drives and inside jokes that only they understood. She missed those moments, missed the version of their friendship that felt effortless and pure.

Her nostalgia was interrupted by an unexpected knock at the door. "Come in," Nia called, expecting Zahara. But when the door opened, it wasn't Zahara standing there—it was Jordan, looking uncertain but determined.

His visit led to an emotionally charged conversation where he admitted his fear of being left behind, while Nia reassured him that although their relationship was changing, it didn't mean they would lose each other entirely. The conversation brought a tentative sense of closure, a fragile truce between them as they navigated the shifting landscape of their friendship. After Jordan left, Zahara returned and immediately noticed the change in Nia's mood, teasing her about the drama and earning a laugh from Nia, who finally felt like she could breathe again. Though far from resolved, the evening left her feeling lighter, more hopeful, and ready to face whatever came next.

The next morning, Nia woke up to the sound of Zahara bustling around the dorm, muttering to herself about a lost notebook. Nia groaned, pulling the blanket over her head, but Zahara wasn't having it. "Get up, sleepyhead. We've got class, and I am not letting you mope around today," Zahara declared, yanking the blanket away with a grin.

"I'm not moping," Nia mumbled, sitting up and rubbing her eyes. "I'm processing."

Zahara raised an eyebrow, unimpressed. "Processing what? That Jordan has feelings, too? Welcome to the club. Now, get dressed. Coffee's on me."

Nia sighed but smiled, grateful for Zahara's relentless energy. As much as she hated to admit it, she needed the push.

By the time they reached the campus coffee shop, the morning rush was in full swing. Students crowded around the counter, chatting about assignments and weekend plans. Nia scanned the room, half-expecting to see Jordan, but there was no sign of him. Zahara placed their order and handed Nia a steaming cup of coffee, her eyes sparkling mischievously. "So," Zahara began as they found a table near the window, "are we going to talk about the fact that Jordan showed up at our dorm last night, or are we pretending that didn't happen?"

Nia groaned, sinking into her seat. "Do we have to?"

Zahara smirked. "Absolutely. Spill."

Reluctantly, Nia recounted the conversation, her voice low so the surrounding tables couldn't overhear. Zahara listened intently, her expression shifting from amused to thoughtful as Nia described Jordan's fears of being left behind.

"Okay," Zahara said finally, leaning back in her chair. "I get it. He's scared. But you can't let his fear dictate your life. You're here to grow, not to stay stuck in the past."

Nia nodded, her coffee cooling in her hands. "I know that. It's just... complicated. I just don't want to hurt him."

Zahara reached across the table, placing a hand on Nia's. "You're not hurting him by growing, Nia. You're just living your life. He has to figure out how to do the same."

Their conversation was interrupted by the arrival of Leila who waved enthusiastically as she approached. "There you two are!" Leila exclaimed, dropping her bag onto the table. "I've been looking for you everywhere. We have to talk about the group project."

Nia groaned inwardly, having almost forgotten about the looming deadline. Zahara, ever the optimist, smiled and gestured for Leila to sit. "What's the latest?"

Leila launched into a detailed explanation of her ideas, her hands moving animatedly as she spoke. Nia tried to focus, but her mind kept drifting back to Jordan, her thoughts a tangled mess of guilt and frustration.

Later that afternoon, as they worked on their project in the library, Nia's phone buzzed with another message from Jordan. This time, she didn't read it right away, slipping the phone into her pocket instead. She could feel Zahara watching her, but Zahara didn't say anything, for which Nia was grateful. The tension between her and Jordan felt like a weight she couldn't shake, but she knew she needed to set boundaries—for her sake and his.

That evening, Nia found herself wandering the campus alone, her thoughts heavy as she strolled past the familiar landmarks: the fountain where she and Zahara had sat on their first day, the student center buzzing with activity, the quad where she often studied between classes.

As she passed the student center, she heard laughter and music spilling out of the open doors. Curiosity got the better of her, and she peeked inside to see a small group of students gathered for an open mic night. A guy with a guitar was on stage, singing a soulful rendition of a song Nia didn't recognize. She hesitated for a moment before stepping inside and finding a seat near the back. The room was dimly lit, the atmosphere intimate and welcoming. As the next performer took the stage, Nia felt a sense of calm wash over her, the music providing a brief respite from her racing thoughts.

Halfway through the evening, Zahara appeared, spotting Nia and making her way over with a grin. "Figured I'd find you here," Zahara said, plopping down beside her. "You doing okay?"

Nia nodded, her gaze fixed on the stage. "Yeah. Just needed a break."

Zahara studied her for a moment before nodding. "Fair enough. Mind if I join you?"

Nia smiled. "Of course not."

As the night went on, Nia found herself relaxing in Zahara's company, their conversation light and easy. For a little while, she was able to forget about Jordan and the weight of her own doubts. But as they left the student center and made their way back to the dorm, reality began to creep back in.

Zahara, ever perceptive, noticed the shift in Nia's mood. "You're thinking about him again, aren't you?" she asked gently.

Nia sighed, nodding. "I can't help it. It's like no matter what I do, he's always there, in the back of my mind."

Zahara stopped walking, turning to face Nia. "Listen to me," she said firmly. "You're not responsible for his happiness, Nia. You can be there for him, but you can't fix him. He has to do that himself."

Nia nodded, Zahara's words sinking in. She knew her friend was right, but it didn't make it any easier. As they reached their dorm, Nia felt a renewed determination to set boundaries, to focus on herself and the new life she was building. But as she settled into bed that night, her phone buzzed again with another message from Jordan. Again, she didn't open it. Instead, she placed the phone face down on her desk, took a deep breath, and closed her eyes, letting sleep take her.

The next day brought new challenges and distractions. Nia threw herself into her classes and group project, trying to keep her mind occupied. Leila's enthusiasm and Zahara's steady presence helped, but the tension with Jordan remained an undercurrent in her thoughts. During a break between classes, Zahara pulled Nia aside, her expression serious. "We need to talk," she said, leading Nia to a quiet corner of the quad.

"What's going on?" Nia asked, her heart sinking.

Zahara hesitated, then sighed. "I saw Jordan earlier. He looked... rough. I think he's really struggling."

Nia felt a pang of guilt, but she quickly pushed it aside. "I can't keep focusing all my energy on him, Zahara. I need to focus on myself."

Zahara nodded, her gaze steady. "I get that. But maybe you should talk to him one more time. Set some clear boundaries. Otherwise, this is just going to keep dragging on."

Nia sighed, knowing Zahara was right. "Okay," she said reluctantly. "I'll talk to him."

That evening, Nia sent Jordan a message, asking if they could meet. He responded almost immediately, agreeing to meet at the fountain. As Nia made her way there, her stomach churned with nerves. When she arrived, Jordan was already waiting, his hands shoved into his pockets and his expression guarded.

As Nia walked toward Jordan, she couldn't ignore the nervous fluttering in her stomach. She had been avoiding this conversation for days, but the silence between them had grown too heavy to bear. The air was thick with unspoken tension as she sat down beside him on the bench, the same one they had sat on so many times before. Jordan looked at her, his expression unreadable, as though he, too, had been bracing for this moment. For a few moments, neither of them spoke, the sounds of the campus fading around them as they sat in heavy silence, both waiting for the other to break it. Finally, Nia couldn't take it any longer. "Jordan, we need to talk about everything," she said, her voice steady but quieter than usual.

He shifted slightly, and she could see the hesitation in his eyes. "I know," he replied, his voice hoarse. "I've been thinking about it a lot, too." Nia drew in a deep breath, her fingers fidgeting in her lap. "Look, I didn't mean to push you away or make things worse. I just... I don't know how to manage to help Zahara with her family problems and focus on school.". Her words felt heavy as she spoke them, the weight of her own emotions slipping out of her mouth before she could stop them. She had been bottling it all up for days, and now, finally, it felt like it was spilling out in a rush.

Jordan ran a hand through his hair, looking down at the ground for a moment, clearly struggling to find the right words. "I get it, Nia," he said quietly, his voice laced with guilt. "I really do." He glanced at her.

"I'm sorry it seems as if I'm pushing you away, Jordan. I'm not and I'm going to try my hardest to make sure you don't feel this way again". She said while twirling her hair. She needed him to understand that she wasn't doing this on purpose and that she actually does care for him. They had been friends for a while now, but this was a moment of change, and sometimes change meant painful realizations.

"I'm sorry if I've been selfish," she added softly, her voice tinged with regret. Jordan didn't say anything for a long moment. Instead, he just sat there, staring at his hands as though he couldn't look her in the eye.

Finally, Jordan exhaled deeply, lifting his gaze to meet hers. "I understand Nia," he said, his voice quieter now. "I've been inconsiderate and not realizing that you've been busy with school and helping Zahara. I know you have a lot on your plate... I just don't want you to forget about me."

His words hit her like a wave, and the first time in days, she felt the pressure in her chest ease. Nia felt a pang of guilt in her chest. She hadn't meant to hurt him, but at the same time, she knew she couldn't keep ignoring her own needs. "You're not going to lose me, Jordan," she said, her tone reassuring, though her heart wasn't entirely convinced. They sat there in silence for a few more moments, the weight of the conversation lingering in the air. Nia wasn't sure what the future held for them, but she knew that she couldn't continue this cycle of trying to save him at the cost of her own well-being.

Maybe they would both figure things out or maybe they

wouldn't. Either way, it felt like a crossroads.

Finally, Jordan spoke again, his voice tinged with a hint of relief. "I understand, Nia. I'm sorry for everything. I'll figure it out. I promise."

Nia nodded, a small smile tugging at her lips. "I hope so, Jordan. I really do."

The conversation was difficult, both of them struggling to find the right words. Nia explained that she needed space to focus on herself and her new life, while Jordan admitted that he was afraid of losing her. They both cried, their emotions raw and unfiltered, but by the end of it, they reached an understanding. It wasn't a perfect resolution, but it was a start.

As they stood up from the bench, Nia felt a strange sense of finality. This wasn't the end, not exactly, but it was a turning point. Their friendship had changed, and she couldn't pretend otherwise. It was no longer just about her and him—it was about both of them learning to stand on their own, apart from each other, even if they would always care for one another. Walking back to her dorm, Nia felt the heaviness of the past few days lift, replaced by a quiet sense of clarity. The road ahead wasn't clear, and she didn't know what the future held for her and Jordan, but at least she knew that she was finally putting herself first. And that, she thought, was enough.

Chapter 7
Unsteady Ground

The morning sun crept through the blinds of Nia's dorm room, casting long golden streaks on the walls. She lay in bed, staring at the ceiling, replaying her conversation with Jordan over and over in her mind. There was relief in having spoken her truth, but there was also a new kind of emptiness—a space where their friendship had once been so easy, now occupied by uncertainty. Zahara's soft breathing from across the room was the only sound. Nia turned her head, watching her roommate as she slept peacefully, seemingly unbothered by the chaos in Nia's world. She envied Zahara's ability to stay grounded, no matter what life threw her way. Nia wished she could borrow even a fraction of Zahara's composure.

Nia's phone buzzed on her nightstand, breaking the stillness. She reached for it, half expecting another message from Jordan, but instead, it was Leila: *Hey, can we meet today to work on our part of the presentation? Chris is being useless, and I don't want to wait until the last minute.*

Nia sighed, sitting up and running a hand through her messy

hair. Leila was blunt, almost to a fault, but Nia appreciated her no-nonsense approach to their project. It was better than the passive-aggressive texts Chris had been sending all week, complaining about how much work he had while contributing next to nothing.

Sure, what time? Nia texted back, setting the phone down as she swung her legs over the edge of the bed. She had planned to spend the day decompressing, maybe taking a walk or journaling to clear her head, but she knew she couldn't afford to fall behind. College was proving to be a delicate balancing act, and every time she thought she had things under control, something new tipped the scales.

By the time Zahara stirred awake, Nia was dressed and halfway through an apple she had grabbed from the mini-fridge. "You're up early," Zahara mumbled, her voice thick with sleep. She sat up, her curly hair forming a halo around her head. "Everything okay?"

"Yeah," Nia replied, though the tightness in her chest suggested otherwise. "I'm meeting Leila to work on our project. She's stressed about Chris not pulling his weight."

Zahara stretched, her arms reaching high above her head. "Classic group project problems. You want me to come for moral support?"

Nia smiled, appreciating the offer, but shook her head. "Thanks, but I think I've got it. Besides, you've got your own stuff to do."

Zahara nodded, her expression thoughtful. "Well, if you need a break later, let me know. We could grab dinner or something."

"Sounds good," Nia said, grabbing her backpack. "See you later."

The walk to the library was brisk, the cool autumn air biting at her cheeks. The campus buzzed with activity—students rushing to classes, groups gathered on the quad, laughter and chatter filling the air. It was a stark contrast to the solitude Nia felt as she weaved through the crowd. She found Leila at their usual spot near the back of the library, already surrounded by textbooks, notes, and her laptop.

"Hey," Leila said, barely looking up as Nia sat down. "I've been trying to organize our section, but Chris hasn't sent me anything. I swear, he's just waiting for us to do all the work."

Nia nodded, pulling out her own notes. "Yeah, I noticed. I messaged him last night, but all he said was that he's *busy*.'" She made air quotes, earning a snort from Leila.

"Of course he's busy," Leila said sarcastically. "Probably playing video games or something. Whatever, we'll just have to carry him. Again."

They spent the next couple of hours piecing together their portion of the presentation, bouncing ideas off each other and refining their slides. Despite Leila's sharp tongue, she was efficient and focused, and Nia found herself grateful to have her as a partner. By the time they wrapped up, Nia felt a sense of accomplishment, even if it was tinged with annoyance at Chris's lack of effort.

"Thanks for sticking with this," Nia said as they packed up. "I know it's frustrating."

Leila shrugged. "It is what it is. Just remind me never to work with seniors again. They've already checked out."

As they parted ways, Nia felt a bit lighter. The project was far from finished, but they had made progress, and that was something. She decided to take Zahara up on her offer for dinner, shooting her a quick text as she headed back to the dorm.

When she arrived, Zahara was already waiting, dressed in a casual yet stylish outfit that made Nia feel underdressed in her sweatshirt and jeans. "Where do you want to go?" Zahara asked, slinging her bag over her shoulder.

"Anywhere that's not the dining hall," Nia replied with a laugh. "I can't eat another slice of cardboard pizza."

They settled on a cozy café just off campus, a place Zahara had discovered during her first week. The smell of fresh bread and coffee greeted them as they walked in, and Nia felt a wave of comfort wash over her. They ordered sandwiches and sat by the window, watching the world go by as they ate.

"So," Zahara said, her tone casual but curious, "how are you feeling after everything with Jordan?"

Nia hesitated, taking a bite of her sandwich to buy herself time. "I don't know," she admitted finally. "I think I did the right thing, but it still feels... weird.

Zahara nodded, her gaze thoughtful. "Change is hard, especially when it comes to people you care about. But sometimes it's necessary, you know?

Nia smiled, grateful for Zahara's unwavering support. "You're right. It's just going to take some time to adjust."

They spent the rest of the evening talking about lighter topics—classes, upcoming events, and Zahara's latest photography project. By the time they returned to the dorm, Nia felt more at ease, her earlier anxieties pushed to the back of her mind.

But as she lay in bed that night, staring at the ceiling once again, her thoughts drifted back to Jordan. She wondered if he was okay if he had taken their conversation to heart. She hoped he would find his way, just as she was trying to find hers.

For now, though, she knew she had to focus on herself. And for the first time in a long time, that felt like enough.

Nia woke up the next morning to the sound of Zahara bustling around the room, packing her camera bag with practiced efficiency. "Big plans today?" Nia mumbled, rubbing the sleep from her eyes.

"Yeah, I'm heading to the art building to work on my photography project," Zahara replied without looking up. "There's this old part of campus with these gorgeous stone archways, and I've been dying to shoot there while the morning light's good."

Nia stretched, a yawn escaping her lips. "You're so dedicated. I can't remember the last time I felt that excited about something."

Zahara glanced at her, a small smile tugging at the corner of her mouth. "Maybe you just haven't found your thing yet. Don't worry, it'll come."

As Zahara zipped up her bag and headed out, Nia couldn't help but feel a twinge of jealousy. Zahara always seemed so sure of herself, so driven. Nia, on the other hand, still felt like she was fumbling her way through college, unsure of where she fit in or what she wanted.

She spent the next hour slowly getting ready, her mind drifting to the growing pile of assignments on her desk. She knew she should dive into her work, but the thought of spending another day cooped up in the library felt unbearable. Instead, she grabbed her notebook and decided to head to the campus fountain—a spot she'd come to love for its calming atmosphere and the way the sound of running water drowned out her racing thoughts.

When she arrived, the fountain was surrounded by students, some chatting in small groups while others sat alone, lost in their own worlds. Nia found an empty bench and sat down, opening her notebook to a blank page. She stared at it for a moment, unsure of what to write. Journaling had always been her way of processing her feelings, but lately, even her thoughts felt too tangled to put into words.

She was lost in thought when a familiar voice broke through her reverie. "Hey."

Nia looked up to see Jordan standing a few feet away, his hands stuffed into his jacket pockets. He looked hesitant, almost like he wasn't sure if he should be there.

"Hey," Nia replied, her voice neutral. She closed her notebook, unsure of what to expect from this conversation.

"Can I sit?" Jordan asked, nodding toward the bench.

Nia hesitated for a moment before nodding. "Sure."

Jordan sat down, leaving a noticeable gap between them. For a moment, neither of them spoke, the sound of the fountain filling the silence.

"I've been thinking a lot about what you said," Jordan began, his voice quiet. "About how I've been taking you for granted."

Nia glanced at him, surprised by the vulnerability in his tone. "And?"

"And you were right," he admitted, meeting her gaze. "I've been so wrapped up in my own stuff that I didn't stop to think about how it was affecting you. I'm sorry, Nia. You didn't deserve that."

Nia felt a mix of emotions—relief, sadness, and a lingering

frustration. "I appreciate you saying that, Jordan. But it's not just about apologizing. It's about actually meaning it, you know?

"I know," Jordan said, his voice steady. "And I really do mean it."

Nia studied him, searching for sincerity in his expression. She wanted to believe him, but a part of her was still guarded.

"Thank you, Nia. For being honest with me. I know it couldn't have been easy." Jordan said in a meaningful way.

"It wasn't," Nia admitted. "But it needed to happen."

They sat in silence for a while, the tension between them easing slightly. It wasn't a perfect resolution, but it felt like a step in the right direction.

After Jordan left, Nia stayed at the fountain for a while longer, her thoughts swirling. She knew rebuilding their friendship would take time, and she wasn't sure if it would ever be the same. But for now, she was content to take things one day at a time.

As the afternoon sun climbed higher in the sky, Nia decided to head to the campus café for a cup of tea. The line was long, but she didn't mind the wait. It gave her time to people-watch, to observe the little moments of connection and humanity that played out all around her.

While she waited, she felt a tap on her shoulder and turned to see Zahara standing behind her, camera slung over one shoulder. "Fancy meeting you here," Zahara said with a grin.

"Hey!" Nia said, her mood lifting instantly. "How was your shoot?"

"Productive," Zahara replied. "But I'm starving. Want to grab a table together?"

"Absolutely," Nia said, grateful for the company.

They found a small table by the window, and Zahara wasted no time diving into her food while Nia sipped her tea. "So," Zahara said between bites, "how's your day been?"

"Eventful," Nia replied, giving her a brief rundown of her conversation with Jordan.

Zahara listened intently, her expression thoughtful. "Sounds like progress," she said when Nia finished. "Even if it's slow, it's something."

"Yeah," Nia agreed. "I just hope it lasts."

"It will," Zahara said confidently. "You're both putting in the effort, and that's what matters."

They spent the rest of their time at the café talking and laughing, the weight of the past few days slowly lifting from Nia's shoulders. By the time they left, she felt lighter and more hopeful.

As they walked back to the dorm, Zahara paused, glancing at Nia. "You know, I think you're stronger than you give yourself credit for."

Nia looked at her, surprised. "What makes you say that?"

"Because you're still here, still pushing forward, even when things get tough," Zahara said. "That takes strength, Nia. Don't forget that."

Nia felt a warmth spread through her chest at Zahara's words. She didn't always feel strong, but in that moment, she realized that maybe she was stronger than she thought.

Back in their dorm room, Nia sat down at her desk, opening her notebook once again. This time, the words came easily, spilling onto the page like a release. She wrote about her conversation with Jordan, about the way Zahara always seemed to know exactly what to say, about the small moments of beauty she had noticed throughout the day.

As she wrote, Nia felt a sense of clarity she hadn't felt in weeks. She didn't have all the answers, and she didn't know what the future held, but she was learning to trust herself, to trust the process. And for the first time in a long time, that felt like enough.

Nia's pen hovered over the page as her thoughts drifted to Zahara's words from earlier: "You're stronger than you give yourself credit for." The warmth she had felt when Zahara said it still lingered, but now it was accompanied by a quiet sense of determination. Maybe Zahara was right. Maybe she had more strength in her than she realized. She just needed to figure out how to tap into it.

The quiet buzz of her phone snapped her out of her reverie. She glanced at the screen to see a text from Jordan: *Hey. Thanks again for today. It meant a lot. Let's talk more soon.*

Nia read the message twice, her feelings a mixture of hope and skepticism. She typed a simple reply—*Sure, talk soon*—and set her phone aside.

She turned her focus back to her notebook. Words began to flow, her pen scratching steadily against the paper as she wrote about the day—the conversation with Jordan, the comforting time spent with Zahara, the way the sunlight filtered through the café window. Writing had always been her way of making sense of the world, and tonight, it felt especially grounding.

Just as she finished her last sentence, Zahara walked into the room, balancing two mugs of tea in her hands. "Thought you could use this," she said, placing one of the mugs on Nia's desk.

Nia smiled, grateful for the gesture. "Thanks. You've been on fire with the supportive friend vibes lately."

Zahara laughed, taking a seat on her bed. "What can I say? I'm a giver. Plus, you've had a lot going on. I figured you could use a little extra TLC."

Nia took a sip of the tea, savoring its warmth. "You're not wrong," she admitted. "Today was... a lot. But it felt good to finally say what I needed to say to Jordan. Even if I'm not sure what's next."

"Sometimes just taking that first step is the hardest part," Zahara said, her tone thoughtful. "You're figuring it out, and that's what matters."

Nia nodded, appreciating Zahara's perspective. She realized how lucky she was to have a roommate who not only understood her but also knew how to encourage her without pushing too hard.

They spent the next hour talking about everything and nothing, the conversation meandering from childhood memories to their favorite music to Zahara's photography project. Nia found herself laughing more than she had in days, and for the first time in a while, she felt a genuine sense of lightness.

Eventually, Zahara yawned and stretched, announcing she was calling it a night. Nia stayed up a little longer, staring at her notebook and thinking about how much had changed since the start of the semester. She still felt like she was finding her footing, but she was starting to believe that maybe, just maybe, she was capable of handling whatever came her way.

The next morning, Nia woke up feeling unusually refreshed. She decided to take advantage of her rare burst of energy by heading to the library to get a jumpstart on her assignments. The library was quiet, the faint hum of the air conditioning the only sound as she found a corner table and spread out her notes.

For the next few hours, Nia worked steadily, immersing herself in her studies. It felt good to be productive, to feel like she was making progress. By the time she packed up her things and headed out, she was in a much better mood than she had been in days.

As she walked across campus, her phone buzzed with a text from Zahara: Meet me at the art building at noon. I have something to show you.

Intrigued, Nia texted back an affirmative and made her way to the art building. She found Zahara in one of the photography studios, her camera and laptop set up on a table.

"Hey," Zahara greeted her with a grin. "Perfect timing. I just finished editing the photos from yesterday, and I wanted you to see them."

Nia leaned over the laptop as Zahara clicked through the images. Each photo was stunning, capturing the beauty of the campus in ways Nia had never noticed before. The soft morning light cast a golden glow over the stone archways, and the intricate details of the architecture seemed to come alive.

"These are amazing," Nia said, genuinely impressed.

"Thanks," Zahara said, her grin widening. "It's crazy how different things can look through a lens. It makes you notice stuff you'd normally overlook."

Nia nodded, feeling a newfound appreciation for Zahara's passion. "You've got such an eye for this. It's inspiring."

Zahara shrugged modestly but looked pleased. "It's just what I love to do. Speaking of which, I was thinking... You said you're still trying to figure out what you're passionate about, right?"

"Yeah," Nia said slowly, wondering where Zahara was going with this.

"Well, what if you tried photography? Just for fun. You might surprise yourself."

Nia hesitated. "I don't know... I've never really been into photography."

"Doesn't mean you can't give it a shot," Zahara said, holding up her camera. "Here, take it. Go outside and play around with it for a bit. No pressure, no expectations. Just see what happens."

Nia looked at the camera, then back at Zahara. She could see the excitement in her friend's eyes, and a part of her couldn't help but be curious. "Okay," she said finally. "I'll give it a try."

Zahara beamed and handed her the camera, giving her a quick rundown of how to use it. Nia stepped outside, feeling a mix of nervousness and excitement as she adjusted the settings and started snapping photos.

At first, she felt awkward, unsure of what to focus on. But as she walked around campus, she began to notice little details she had never paid attention to before—the way the sunlight filtered through the trees, the vibrant colors of the fall leaves, the intricate patterns of shadows on the pavement.

By the time she returned to the studio, Nia was smiling. "I don't know if I'm any good, but that was actually really fun," she admitted, handing the camera back to Zahara.

Zahara grinned. "Told you. Let's take a look at what you got."

They uploaded the photos to Zahara's laptop, and as they scrolled through the images, Nia was surprised to see that a few of them were actually pretty decent.

"You've got potential," Zahara said, her tone encouraging. "If you ever want to learn more, I'm happy to teach you."

Nia felt a spark of excitement she hadn't felt in a long time. Maybe this was something she could explore, something that could help her feel more connected to herself and the world around her.

"Thanks, Zahara," she said sincerely. "I might just take you up on that."

As they left the art building together, Nia felt a sense of possibility she hadn't experienced in weeks. She didn't know where this new interest might lead, but for the first time in a long time, she felt like she was starting to find her way.

Nia woke up the next morning to the soft, golden light streaming through the window. Zahara had already left for an early class, leaving the room quiet except for the faint hum of the air conditioning. The camera Zahara had lent her sat on her desk, a quiet reminder of the new door she'd opened the day before. Nia stared at it for a moment, feeling the mix of excitement and trepidation that always came with trying something new.

She decided to bring the camera with her as she went about her day. Maybe she'd find some inspiration along the way. Slipping it into her bag, she headed out, grabbing her notebook and a snack for later. Her first class was uneventful, though she found herself glancing out the window more often than usual, her mind drifting to the patterns of light and shadow she might be able to capture. By the time the lecture ended, she was itching to take the camera out and start experimenting.

Her opportunity came during her break between classes. The campus was alive with activity, students bustling to and from buildings, but Nia's focus was elsewhere. She wandered around, her camera slung over her shoulder, looking for something that caught her eye. It wasn't long before she stumbled upon a small, tucked-away courtyard she had never noticed before. It was quiet, with a single wooden bench surrounded by blooming flowers and a towering oak tree that cast dappled shadows on the ground.

She started snapping photos, unsure of what exactly she was looking for but trusting her instincts. She played with angles and perspectives, crouching low to capture the texture of the tree bark or tilting the camera upward to frame the sunlight streaming through the branches. Time seemed to slip away as she lost herself in the process. For the first time in what felt like forever, her mind wasn't racing with doubts or anxieties. She was simply present, focused on the moment.

As she reviewed her photos, a small smile crept onto her face. They weren't perfect, but there was something about them that felt genuine like they captured a piece of how she saw the world. She didn't notice someone approaching until a familiar voice broke her concentration.

"Looks like someone's getting serious about this photography thing," Zahara said, leaning against the bench with a grin.

Nia laughed, lowering the camera. "I'm not sure about serious, but I'm definitely having fun with it."

Zahara nodded approvingly. "That's what matters. Mind if I take a look?"

Nia handed over the camera, feeling a bit self-conscious as Zahara scrolled through the photos. Zahara's expression softened as she studied the images. "These are really good, Nia. I mean it. You've got an eye for this."

"Thanks," Nia said, her cheeks warming. "It's kind of weird, though. I've never really thought of myself as creative."

"Maybe you just needed the right medium," Zahara said with a shrug. "Sometimes it takes a while to find what clicks."

They sat together on the bench for a while, talking about everything from photography to their favorite childhood memories. Nia found herself opening up in a way she rarely did with anyone else. Zahara had a way of making her feel seen and understood, and it was a comfort she didn't take for granted.

Later that afternoon, Nia headed to the library to get some studying done. She was halfway through her notes when Jordan appeared, looking sheepish but determined. "Hey," he said, sliding into the chair across from her.

Nia raised an eyebrow, unsure of what to expect. "Hey."

Jordan fiddled with the strap of his backpack, avoiding her gaze. "Hey, how's it going?"

Nia looked up at him "Hey everything's good just a bit busy lately how about you?"

"I bet and I'm just taking stuff day by day," he said quickly.

"I'm not mad at you at all I just want everything to go back to normal."

Nia said reassuringly

Jordan nodded, his expression earnest. "I'm glad you aren't mad at me and yeah let's just let everything go back to normal."

They talked for a while longer, easing into a more comfortable rhythm. By the time Jordan left, Nia felt cautiously optimistic. Maybe things could improve between them.

The rest of the week passed in a blur of classes, studying, and stolen moments with her camera. Nia found herself looking forward to her breaks when she could wander the campus and capture little snippets of life through her lens. She even started experimenting with editing, sitting with Zahara in the art building as they worked side by side.

One evening, as they were going through photos together, Zahara glanced at Nia with a thoughtful expression. "You know, there's a student art showcase coming up next month. You should think about submitting something."

Nia's eyes widened. "Me? No way. I'm not good enough for that."

"Don't sell yourself short," Zahara said firmly. "You've got talent, Nia. And more importantly, you've got a unique perspective. That's what art is about."

The idea both excited and terrified her. She had never considered sharing her work with others, let alone in such a public way. But as she thought about it, she realized it might be exactly what she needed—a chance to push herself, to step outside her comfort zone.

"I'll think about it," she said finally, and Zahara smiled, satisfied.

The next morning, Nia woke up to a text from her mom, asking how she was doing. She hesitated before replying, unsure of how to explain the whirlwind of emotions she'd been experiencing. Instead, she kept it simple: I'm doing okay. Figuring things out, little by little.

Her mom's response came quickly: Proud of you. Call me when you have time.

Nia felt a pang of guilt for not keeping in touch as much as she should have, but she promised herself she'd call that evening. For now, she had a full day ahead of her, and she was determined to make the most of it.

As she headed to class, camera in tow, Nia felt a sense of purpose she hadn't felt in a long time. She didn't have all the answers, and she knew there would be challenges ahead, but for the first time, she felt like she was on the right path.

The late afternoon sun bathed the campus in a warm, golden

glow as Nia wrapped up her final class of the day. She clutched her notebook tightly as she exited the lecture hall, her mind still buzzing with the professor's explanations of nonverbal communication. Despite her initial struggles to adjust to the pace of college, she felt herself slowly finding her footing. The information didn't feel quite as overwhelming anymore, and for the first time, she even managed to answer a question in class without her voice shaking. It wasn't much, but it was a step forward—one she felt proud of.

Nia decided to head to the library to review her notes and get a jumpstart on her upcoming assignments. As she walked, she felt the familiar weight of the camera in her bag. Lately, she had been carrying it with her everywhere, almost like a talisman. Photography had become her solace, a way to express herself without having to rely on words she often struggled to find.

She arrived at the library and found a quiet corner by the window. The view overlooked a small garden that was filled with students lounging on the grass or chatting on benches. Nia pulled out her camera, feeling a spark of inspiration. She adjusted the lens and began snapping pictures, experimenting with the lighting and angles. There was something therapeutic about the act of framing a shot, about capturing a fleeting moment and freezing it in time.

As she reviewed the images on the small screen, she noticed a few that stood out—a couple laughing together under a tree, a student absorbed in a book with sunlight streaming over the pages, and a squirrel perched on the edge of a bench, seemingly posing for the camera. A small smile tugged at her lips. These were the kinds of moments she wanted to remember, the small, quiet joys that often went unnoticed.

Her focus was broken when Zahara texted her: *You free for dinner?*

Nia glanced at the time and realized it was already past six. She quickly packed up her things and replied: *Meet me at the dining hall in 10?*

When she arrived, Zahara was already waiting by the entrance, her arms crossed and a mischievous grin on her face.

"You've got your camera, don't you?" Zahara asked, gesturing toward the bag slung over Nia's shoulder.

"Of course," Nia said, laughing. "Why?"

"Because after we eat, I'm taking you to my favorite spot on campus. Trust me, it's going to blow your mind."

Intrigued, Nia agreed, and they headed inside. Over plates of pasta and salad, Zahara filled Nia in on her day, sharing stories about her classes and the amusing antics of her photography club. Nia listened intently, feeling grateful for Zahara's friendship. She hadn't realized how much she had been missing a connection like this—someone who understood her without judgment and encouraged her to be herself.

After dinner, Zahara led Nia across campus, weaving through pathways Nia had never ventured down before. The sun had set by now, and the campus was illuminated by the soft glow of streetlights and the occasional lamp in a dormitory window. Zahara finally stopped at the edge of a small hill that overlooked the city. Below them, the skyline stretched out in a glittering expanse, the lights twinkling like stars against the inky darkness.

"This is where I come when I need to clear my head," Zahara said, her voice quieter now. "Something about the view just makes everything feel... smaller, you know? Like all the stuff I'm worried about isn't as big as it seems."

Nia nodded, her breath catching as she took in the sight. She pulled out her camera, adjusting the settings to capture the scene in front of her. The city lights reflected in the lens, creating a dazzling effect that she knew would translate beautifully in the photo. Zahara sat beside her, leaning back on her hands and gazing out at the horizon.

"You should come here more often," Zahara said after a while. "It's good for the soul."

"I think I will," Nia replied, lowering her camera and letting the view soak in. "Thanks for showing me this."

Zahara smiled. "Anytime."

They sat in comfortable silence for a while, the only sounds the distant hum of traffic and the rustling of leaves in the breeze. Nia felt a sense of peace she hadn't experienced in weeks. For the first time, she didn't feel the weight of her doubts pressing down on her. She was here, in this moment, and that was enough.

When they finally decided to head back, the walk to their dorm was filled with lighthearted chatter. Zahara told Nia about a new project she was working on, and Nia shared her tentative plans to submit a photo to the upcoming art showcase. Zahara's enthusiasm was infectious, and by the time they reached their room, Nia felt a renewed sense of determination.

As they settled in for the night, Zahara turned to Nia. "You know, I think you're really starting to find your groove here."

Nia looked at her friend, surprised by the comment. "You think so?"

"Definitely," Zahara said with a nod. "You're putting yourself out there, trying new things, and figuring out what makes you happy. That's what college is all about."

Nia smiled, her heart swelling with gratitude. "Thanks, Zahara. That means a lot."

The next morning, Nia woke up early, feeling a burst of energy she hadn't felt in a long time. She decided to go for a walk before her first class, bringing her camera with her as usual. The campus was quiet, the morning light casting long shadows across the ground. She wandered through the pathways, snapping photos of anything that caught her eye.

She ended up back at the courtyard she had discovered earlier in the week. Sitting on the bench, she reviewed her photos, feeling a sense of accomplishment. Each image was a small victory, a testament to her growth and resilience.

As she sat there, she realized something important: she didn't have to have everything figured out right away. College was a journey, and it was okay to take it one step at a time. She would have doubts and setbacks, but she would also have moments of joy and connection—moments like this.

Nia packed up her camera and headed to class, her steps lighter than they had been in weeks. She didn't know what the future held, but for the first time, she felt ready to embrace it. Whatever came her way, she knew she had the strength to face it. And that was enough.

Chapter 8
Her Lens

The morning sun painted the campus in soft hues of gold, and Nia wandered its pathways with her camera in hand. She had started this habit tentatively at first, unsure if she could truly capture the beauty she saw. But now, it had become her morning ritual—a quiet escape before the bustle of the day took over. Her sneakers crunched on the gravel paths as she explored the familiar yet suddenly fascinating world around her.

The ivy that clung to the brick dormitory walls caught her eye, the sunlight filtering through its leaves creating intricate patterns of shadow. She raised her camera and adjusted the settings Zahara had shown her, focusing on the play of light and texture. The click of the shutter felt satisfying, almost like a secret she was capturing to keep for herself.

From there, she moved toward the library, where the massive windows reflected the soft blue of the morning sky. She crouched low to capture the symmetrical patterns in the reflection, her mind quiet and focused. Nearby, a few students passed, chatting and laughing, but their noise felt distant, like background music to her creative solitude.

As she walked, Nia began to notice things she'd never paid attention to before: the way fallen leaves formed swirling patterns on the pavement, the symmetry of the lampposts lining the quad, and even the texture of an old bench that had clearly weathered years of use. Photography was changing how she saw the world, sharpening her focus on the small, meaningful details she'd once ignored.

During one of her explorations, she stumbled upon a small, hidden garden tucked behind the science building. It wasn't much—a patch of greenery with a single bench and a towering tree whose branches created a canopy overhead. But something about it felt magical, like she'd uncovered a secret. The dappled light filtered through the leaves, creating a mosaic of shadows on the ground. She adjusted her camera settings, remembering Zahara's tips, and snapped several photos from different angles, experimenting with perspective and focus.

That evening, Nia sat cross-legged on her bed, her laptop balanced precariously on a pillow as she scrolled through the photos she had taken. Zahara was on her own bed, flipping through a photography book she had borrowed from the library.

"Hey, can I show you something?" Nia asked hesitantly, tilting her screen toward Zahara.

Zahara looked up, her curiosity piqued, and crawled over to sit beside Nia. "Let's see it," she said, nudging Nia's arm playfully.

Nia clicked through the photos, stopping on one of the garden. It was her favorite—a shot where the sunlight streaming through the branches cast soft, dancing shadows on the bench below.

"Wow," Zahara said, her eyes lighting up. "This is gorgeous. You've got such a natural eye for light and composition. Look at the way the shadows frame the bench—it's like you captured the mood of the whole place."

Nia's cheeks warmed at the compliment. "Really? I wasn't sure if it was any good. I just... liked how it looked."

Zahara grinned, leaning closer to examine the photo in detail. "Exactly. That's what makes it good. You saw something that resonated with you, and you captured it. Photography isn't just about what's in the frame—it's about what it makes you feel."

They spent the rest of the evening reviewing Nia's photos. Zahara critiqued them with the precision of someone who cared deeply about her craft, pointing out where the focus could be sharper or the composition more dynamic. But she also celebrated the moments where Nia's instincts shone through.

"You've got a knack for this," Zahara said as she handed Nia's laptop back. "But now it's time to level up."

Nia raised an eyebrow. "Level up?"

Zahara grabbed her own camera from her desk and plopped down beside Nia. "I'm going to show you how to use manual settings. Auto mode is great for starting out, but if you want to really control how your photos turn out, you need to know how to do it yourself."

For the next hour, Zahara patiently walked Nia through the basics of aperture, shutter speed, and ISO. She explained how each setting influenced the light and mood of a photo, and how they worked together to create the perfect shot.

Nia's head spun with all the new information, but Zahara's excitement was contagious. They practiced with random objects in the room—a desk lamp, a stack of books, even the half-eaten bag of chips on Zahara's nightstand.

By the time they called it a night, Nia felt like she had taken her first real step into the world of photography. Zahara's guidance and encouragement had not only taught her technical skills but also made her feel part of something larger—a shared passion for capturing the world in a way that only they could see.

As she lay in bed, staring at the ceiling, Nia thought about what Zahara had said earlier: "Photography isn't just about what's in the frame—it's about what it makes you feel." She closed her eyes, her mind replaying the quiet moments in the garden, the way the sunlight danced through the branches.

For the first time, she felt like she was starting to find her voice—not through words, but through the images she captured. And for the first time, that felt like enough.

The café was bustling with activity when Nia met Jordan one quiet afternoon. The hum of espresso machines and the low murmur of conversations filled the space as they sat by the window, two mismatched mugs of coffee between them. Nia fiddled with the strap of her camera bag, debating whether to share her photos.

"I see you've been glued to that thing lately," Jordan said, nodding toward her bag. His tone was light, but there was genuine curiosity in his eyes.

Nia smiled sheepishly. "Yeah, I guess I have been. I've been trying to learn more about photography. It's... sort of become my thing."

"Can I see?" he asked, leaning forward slightly.

The request caught her off guard. She hesitated, unsure of how he would react. But something about the way he asked—earnest and without judgment—made her reach for her camera.

"Okay, but don't laugh," she said as she pulled it out and began flipping through her recent shots. She handed him the camera, her palms slightly clammy.

Jordan held it carefully, scrolling through her photos. He stopped on one of her favorites: the garden with the dappled sunlight on the bench.

"This is amazing, Nia," he said, his voice quiet but sincere.

She blinked, caught off guard. "You think so?"

"Yeah," he said, handing the camera back to her. "You've got a great eye for this stuff. It's like... you're capturing more than just what's there. It feels like there's a story behind it."

The compliment warmed her chest, and for the first time in a long time, she felt truly seen.

They spent the rest of their coffee break talking about her photos. Jordan asked thoughtful questions—what inspired her, how she chose her subjects, and what she hoped to convey through her work. Nia found herself opening up more than she expected, sharing how photography had become a way for her to process her emotions and see the world differently.

"Honestly," she admitted, "it's been grounding for me. It's helped me feel less... lost."

Jordan nodded, his expression pensive. "I get that. I've been feeling a little lost myself lately."

She tilted her head, surprised by his vulnerability. "Really? Why?"

He shrugged, stirring the coffee in his mug. "I don't know. I guess I've been stuck in this cycle—doing what I'm supposed to do, but not really knowing why. Like, what's the point of it all?"

Nia nodded slowly, understanding more than she expected to. "I think everyone feels that way sometimes. But maybe that's why it's important to find something that grounds you—something that reminds you why you care."

Their conversation lingered in her mind long after they parted ways.

Over the next few weeks, Jordan began joining Nia on her photography outings. At first, she was unsure of how it would work—photography had always felt like a solitary escape for her. But Jordan's presence was surprisingly easy, his quiet encouragement and occasional suggestions adding something new to the experience.

One crisp autumn afternoon, they wandered to a part of campus Nia rarely visited. The late-afternoon sun hung low in the sky, casting everything in a golden glow. Nia stopped to photograph a tree whose branches were bare but still striking against the blue sky. Jordan stood nearby, watching her work.

"You should take a picture of that," he said, nodding toward a nearby railing where the light hit just right.

Nia turned, considering it. "Why?"

"Because it's simple, but it's beautiful," he said, leaning casually against the railing himself.

She raised her camera, framing the shot. Through the lens, she saw him in a way she hadn't before—the soft light highlighting the curve of his jaw, the relaxed confidence in his posture. She hesitated for a moment, then clicked the shutter.

When she lowered the camera, she found him smiling at her. "What?" she asked, feeling slightly self-conscious.

"Nothing," he said with a shrug. "You just look happy when you're behind that camera."

Nia couldn't help but smile back. "I guess I am."

Their outings became a regular thing, and with each one, their conversations grew deeper. One evening, as they sat on a low stone wall overlooking the quad, Jordan opened up about his struggles in a way he never had before.

"I feel like I've been coasting," he admitted, staring out at the students walking below. "Like I'm just going through the motions because it's easier than figuring out what I actually want."

Nia thought for a moment before replying. "Maybe that's okay for now. Not everyone has everything figured out all the time. Sometimes just trying is enough."

He glanced at her, a small smile tugging at his lips. "When did you get so wise?"

She laughed softly. "Probably when I started wandering around with a camera and seeing the world differently."

Their friendship, once strained and uncertain, began to feel solid again—stronger, even. They shared laughs over awkward photos she had taken while experimenting with settings and quiet moments where words weren't necessary.

During one of their outings, Nia captured another photo of Jordan, this time from a different perspective. He was standing under a tree, the golden hour light filtering through the branches. His profile was framed perfectly by the sun's glow, and his expression held a quiet thoughtfulness that felt raw and real.

When she showed him the photo later, he stared at it for a long moment before speaking. "It's weird, seeing yourself like that," he said.

"Do you like it?" she asked, unsure of what he was thinking.

He nodded slowly. "Yeah. I think I do. It feels... honest."

Nia realized then how much she valued his presence in her life. Through photography, she was beginning to see not just the beauty in the world around her but also in the people she cared about—and in herself.

Their relationship, once filled with hesitations and unspoken tensions, had grown into something more. It wasn't just friendship—it was a connection built on shared vulnerability, laughter, and trust. As they walked back to campus that evening, the light fading into twilight, Nia felt a quiet sense of contentment.

For the first time in a long time, she wasn't afraid of where their relationship might go. Instead, she was simply grateful for the moments they were creating together—one frame, one laugh, and one shared silence at a time.

Zahara perched on the edge of her bed, flipping through Nia's latest collection of photos on the laptop. Her face was serious, eyes narrowed in concentration as she examined each image. "This one," she said, pointing to a photo of sunlight streaming through an old windowpane. "It's nice, but what's the story here?"

Nia frowned, leaning over to look. "The light, the patterns... I thought it was about the way they draw you in."

"It's a start," Zahara said with a small smile. "But remember what we talked about—every photo should say something. Ask yourself why it matters. What are you trying to make people feel?"

They had been working like this for weeks, Zahara pushing Nia to think deeper about her work. It wasn't just about snapping pretty pictures anymore—it was about creating something meaningful, something that resonated. Zahara's critiques, though pointed, always came with encouragement. She believed in Nia's potential, and she wasn't going to let her settle for less.

"I think you're ready to tell a story," Zahara said, closing the laptop with a decisive snap. "Go through your portfolio. Find the photos that mean the most to you. Show me how they fit together."

For the next several days, Nia combed through hundreds of images, trying to identify a common thread. She pulled out photos of Zahara laughing under the campus oak tree, Jordan leaning against a railing in golden light, and a candid shot of two students sharing a quiet conversation by the library fountain. As she reviewed them, a pattern emerged—a story about connection, growth, and the small moments that make life feel full.

Late one night, after hours of arranging and rearranging her chosen shots, Nia presented the series to Zahara. "This is it," she said, spreading the prints across her desk. "It's about the relationships that have shaped me here—the ones that have helped me grow."

Zahara studied the photos, her lips curling into a proud smile. "This is beautiful, Nia. It's honest. It's you."

The praise filled Nia with a sense of pride, but also anxiety. With the student art showcase just weeks away, the pressure to refine and perfect her work felt suffocating.

As the showcase approached, Nia's days blurred into a chaotic cycle of classes, assignments, and late nights editing her photos. She spent hours tweaking lighting, cropping edges, and debating over which shots to include. Her academic work began to pile up, with essays and projects looming over her. Sleep became a luxury she couldn't afford.

One evening, Zahara walked into the dorm to find Nia hunched over her laptop, headphones on, her desk littered with empty coffee cups. "Hey," Zahara said, setting her camera bag down. "You've been at this all day. Take a break."

"I can't," Nia replied without looking up. "There's still so much to do."

Zahara frowned, stepping closer. "You're going to burn yourself out. Let me help—"

"I don't need help!" Nia snapped, her voice sharper than she intended. She immediately regretted it but couldn't bring herself to apologize.

Zahara's expression hardened. "Fine. Do it yourself, then." She grabbed her camera bag and left the room, the door clicking shut behind her.

The silence that followed was deafening. Nia sat back in her chair, guilt pooling in her stomach. She knew Zahara had only been trying to help, but the stress of everything had boiled over.

For the next day, tension lingered between them. Zahara gave Nia space, retreating to the library or photography studio instead of staying in their room. The absence of her usual chatter and support left Nia feeling hollow.

During one particularly sleepless night, Nia sat on her bed, staring at the photos she had spread out across her desk. She realized that the very relationships she was trying to celebrate through her work were being strained by her inability to balance her life. Zahara had been there for her every step of the way, and Nia had let her frustration get in the way of that.

The next morning, Nia found Zahara in the common room, scrolling through her phone. "Hey," Nia said quietly, sitting down beside her.

Zahara glanced up but didn't say anything.

"I'm sorry," Nia continued, her voice trembling slightly. "I've been so stressed, and I took it out on you. That wasn't fair."

Zahara sighed, setting her phone aside. "I get it. Stress does that to people. But, Nia, you don't have to do this alone. I'm here to help. We're a team, remember?"

The words hit Nia harder than she expected, and she nodded, her throat tight with emotion. "Thank you. I'll do better, I promise."

Zahara smiled, her usual warmth returning. "Good. Because this showcase is going to be amazing, and you're going to kill it."

With their friendship restored, Zahara helped Nia refocus. They worked together to finalize the series for the showcase, Zahara offering constructive feedback and keeping Nia grounded when her perfectionism threatened to take over.

One night, as they reviewed the final edits, Zahara leaned back in her chair and looked at Nia. "You know," she said, "this series isn't just about the people in your life—it's about you. About how you see the world."

Nia thought about that for a moment. She had always struggled to articulate her feelings in words, but through photography, she had found a way to express herself. The photos weren't just about connection—they were about how she was learning to trust herself and let others in.

By the time the showcase was just days away, Nia felt a cautious sense of confidence. It wasn't perfect, but it was hers. And for the first time, that felt like enough.

Through Zahara's support and the challenges they faced, Nia

had learned an invaluable lesson: creativity, like life, thrives on collaboration. And leaning on others didn't make her weaker—it made her stronger.

Nia stared at the photo displayed on her laptop screen—a candid shot of Zahara laughing beneath the sprawling oak tree near their dorm. Sunlight filtered through the leaves, dappling her face in warm, golden light. In the background, just slightly out of focus, Jordan stood holding a leaf to the sunlight, examining it like it held the secrets of the universe. The image had a raw, unpolished quality, but that's what made it feel so real. It wasn't just a photograph—it was a snapshot of her life, a reflection of the relationships that had helped her grow since arriving at college.

"This one," she whispered to herself, her fingers brushing the edges of the screen. "This is the one."

The decision to submit the photo felt monumental, as though she were opening a door to a room she couldn't fully see. The student art showcase was less than two weeks away, and while part of her felt excited to share her work, another part was consumed by doubt. Would people understand what the photo meant? Would they see the story behind it, or would they dismiss it as amateurish? The thought of exposing such a personal piece to public scrutiny made her stomach churn.

Nia sat on her bed, staring at the photo, when Zahara walked in. Her camera bag was slung over her shoulder, and her hair was tied back in a loose bun. She stopped mid-step when she saw Nia's expression.

"Uh-oh," Zahara said, dropping her bag onto the floor. "That's the face of someone spiraling. What's going on?"

"I think I know which photo I want to submit," Nia said hesitantly, tilting the screen toward Zahara.

Zahara leaned in, her eyes lighting up as she studied the image. "Nia, this is incredible. It's personal, it's authentic—it tells a story and it's me! You've got to submit this."

"You really think it's good enough?" Nia asked, her voice tinged with uncertainty.

Zahara sat beside her, crossing her legs. "It's not just good enough—it's you. And that's what people connect with. Art isn't about being perfect; it's about being real. And this? This is real."

Despite Zahara's reassurance, Nia's self-doubt lingered. She spent hours tweaking the photo, adjusting the lighting and cropping the edges, trying to make it look "worthy" of the showcase. Every time she thought she was finished, she'd find something else to fix. Late one night, as she hovered over her laptop, Jordan texted her.

Jordan: *Late-night editing session?*

Nia: *How'd you guess?*

Jordan: *Because you stress over stuff too much. Want some company?*

Nia hesitated for a moment before replying.

Nia: *Sure.*

Fifteen minutes later, there was a knock on her door. Zahara had gone to bed early, so the room was quiet as Nia let Jordan in. He brought two mugs of tea, handing one to her with a grin.

"You look like you need this," he said, settling into the chair at her desk.

"Thanks," she said, taking a sip. The warmth of the tea was soothing, but her nerves were still frayed.

"So," Jordan said, nodding toward her laptop. "Show me what you're working on."

Nia hesitated, but then she opened the photo on her screen. Jordan leaned closer, his brow furrowing slightly as he studied it.

"This is amazing," he said after a moment. "You've captured something here—like, it's not just a picture. It feels alive."

His words made her heart ache in the best way. "I'm scared it's not enough," she admitted quietly. "What if no one gets it? What if they think it's... I don't know, basic?"

Jordan shook his head. "Who cares what they think? You're putting yourself out there, and that takes guts. Honestly, seeing you go all-in on this photography thing has been inspiring. It's made me want to figure out my own stuff again."

"What do you mean?" Nia asked, curious.

Jordan shrugged, running a hand through his hair. "I used to love writing, you know? Short stories, poetry—stuff like that.

But somewhere along the way, I stopped. Watching you dive into photography... it's reminded me of how much I miss it. So, yeah, you're inspiring, even if you don't see it."

His words settled over her like a warm blanket, easing some of her tension. "Thanks, Jordan. That means a lot."

"Anytime," he said with a smile. "Now, let's get this photo submission-ready."

Over the next few days, Nia leaned on both Zahara and Jordan to finalize the photo. Zahara offered technical advice, helping Nia adjust the composition to make the image even more striking. Jordan, meanwhile, provided emotional support, keeping her grounded when her anxiety threatened to take over.

"You're overthinking it again," Zahara said one afternoon as Nia debated whether the shadows in the background were too distracting.

"I just want it to be perfect," Nia replied, frustrated.

Zahara placed a hand on her shoulder. "Perfect doesn't exist, Nia. What matters is that it's honest. And this is honest."

Finally, the night before the submission deadline, Nia uploaded the photo. Her hands trembled as she clicked the final button to submit. The confirmation email popped up on her screen, and she exhaled deeply, a mix of relief and nerves coursing through her.

"You did it," Zahara said, leaning back in her chair with a grin.

"I did it," Nia repeated, the realization sinking in.

That evening, as she lay in bed, Nia thought about the journey that had brought her to this point. Photography had started as a way to process her emotions, a personal escape from the chaos of college life. But now, it had become something more—a way to connect with others, to tell stories, and to explore who she was.

The next morning, Jordan met her outside the dining hall. "How's it feel?" he asked, falling into step beside her.

"Terrifying," she admitted. "But also... good. Like I did something that matters."

He smiled at her, his gaze warm. "You did. And I can't wait to see it on display."

As they walked toward their first class, Nia felt a sense of calm she hadn't expected. The photo was out of her hands now, and while the anxiety still lingered, she was proud of herself for taking the leap.

For the first time in a long time, she felt like she was stepping into who she was meant to be—one frame, one connection, and one courageous decision at a time.

The days leading up to the student art showcase passed in a whirlwind of preparation, nerves, and quiet moments of reflection. Between classes and final tweaks to her submission, Nia found herself thinking about how much had changed since the semester began. She remembered stepping onto campus for the first time, feeling like a small fish in an impossibly big pond, unsure of who she was or what she wanted. Now, things felt different. Photography had become more than just a hobby—it was a way to connect with others and make sense of herself.

One quiet evening, Nia sat by the fountain, her notebook balanced on her lap. She scribbled a few words: I used to think art was about capturing the world. Now I know it's about capturing yourself in the world.

She smiled to herself, the thought feeling like a revelation.

The night of the showcase arrived faster than she expected. Nia stood outside the gallery, her heart pounding in her chest. The building glowed warmly from within, its large windows revealing walls lined with student art. She could see people milling about inside, their faces animated as they discussed the pieces on display.

Jordan appeared beside her, his presence grounding her in the moment. "You ready?" he asked, his voice low and steady.

"Not even a little," she admitted with a nervous laugh.

"Good," he said with a grin. "That means it matters."

Zahara joined them moments later, practically buzzing with excitement. "Let's do this," she said, looping her arm through Nia's. Together, they stepped inside.

The gallery was alive with energy, the air buzzing with excitement and anticipation. Nia scanned the room, taking in the vibrant array of paintings, photographs, and sculptures created by her peers. Each piece seemed to carry its own story, and she felt a mix of awe and intimidation.

Finally, she spotted her photo, displayed near the center of the room. The sight stopped her in her tracks. There it was—Zahara laughing under the tree, Jordan blurred in the background, the sunlight wrapping them both in a golden glow. Seeing it framed and hung on the wall made it feel real in a way it hadn't before.

She approached slowly, her breath catching in her throat. A small plaque beneath the photo read: Connections by Nia Richards.

Her chest swelled with pride and gratitude. This wasn't just a photo—it was a piece of her.

As the evening progressed, more people stopped to view her work. Some lingered, smiling softly, while others paused in thoughtful silence. Nia found herself watching their reactions, her nerves gradually giving way to a quiet sense of validation.

"Look at this one," a woman said to her companion, gesturing to Nia's photo. "It's so intimate, like you're part of the moment. You can feel the joy and connection."

The comment sent a wave of warmth through Nia. She hadn't expected people to understand her work so deeply, and hearing it out loud felt like a gift.

Jordan and Zahara were never far, each playing their role in supporting her. Jordan hovered near the snack table, occasionally catching her eye and flashing an encouraging smile. Zahara, meanwhile, flitted between groups of people, shamelessly promoting Nia's work to anyone who would listen.

"Have you seen that one over there?" Zahara said to a couple admiring a nearby sculpture. "The photographer's a friend of mine. She's crazy talented."

Nia shook her head, laughing quietly. Leave it to Zahara to be her unofficial PR agent.

Later in the evening, Nia's parents arrived, their faces lighting up when they saw her photo. Her mom pulled her into a tight hug. "We're so proud of you," she said, her voice thick with emotion.

Her dad nodded, his expression softer than usual. "You've got a gift, kiddo. Keep at it."

The presence of her family made the night even more special. They stood by her side, pointing out their favorite elements of the photo and asking about the process behind it. Nia realized then how much their support meant to her, even if she hadn't always acknowledged it.

As the event began to wind down, Nia stood back, taking it all in. The gallery, now quieter, felt almost reverent. Her friends and family gathered around her photo, their laughter and conversation weaving together in a way that mirrored the connection she had tried to capture.

Jordan approached her, hands in his pockets. "How are you feeling?" he asked.

"Lighter," she said, smiling at him. "Like I'm exactly where I'm supposed to be."

He grinned. "I'd say you are."

They stood in comfortable silence for a moment before Jordan spoke again. "Nia, I just want to say... I'm really proud of you. Watching you chase this, put yourself out there—it's been amazing. You inspire me."

Her heart swelled at his words. "Thank you, Jordan. That means more than you know."

Before she could overthink it, she stepped closer, wrapping her arms around him in a hug. He hesitated for a beat, then hugged her back tightly.

As the night drew to a close, Nia found herself standing by her photo one last time, Zahara at her side.

"You did it," Zahara said, nudging her playfully.

Nia nodded, a sense of peace settling over her. "I couldn't have done it without you."

"Damn right you couldn't," Zahara said with a smirk. Then her tone softened. "But seriously, Nia, you should be proud. This isn't just about the photo. It's about everything you've done to get here."

Later, as Nia walked back to the dorm with Jordan and Zahara, the cool night air wrapped around them. Her heart felt full in a way it hadn't in a long time.

She thought about everything the past few months had taught

her—the importance of connection, the power of vulnerability, and the courage it took to chase something meaningful.

Back in her room, Nia sat at her desk, her journal open in front of her. She wrote: Art isn't about being perfect. It's about connection—connecting with others, with yourself, with the world. Tonight, I learned that the courage to be seen is what makes it all worthwhile.

As she set her pen down, she felt a profound sense of accomplishment. Her journey was far from over, but for now, she was exactly where she needed to be. And that was enough.

Chapter 9
The Spotlight

The student art showcase had ended weeks ago, but Nia still carried the memory of seeing her photo displayed with pride. She had moved on to her usual routines—classes, editing her growing portfolio, and meeting Jordan or Zahara for quick meals between their busy schedules. Life felt steady, if a little hectic, until an unexpected email disrupted her day.

Subject: Opportunity to Showcase Your Work
Hi Nia,

My name is Evelyn Brooks, and I'm the curator of The Greenlight Gallery. I recently came across your photo Connections through a mutual contact who attended the student showcase. Your work is incredibly moving, and I would love to discuss the possibility of including it in an upcoming community exhibit.

Please let me know if you're interested.

Best,
Evelyn

Nia reread the email three times, her heart racing with a mix of excitement and disbelief. Someone had noticed her work—someone outside the college bubble. The idea of participating in a gallery exhibit was thrilling, but also daunting. What would it mean to create something for a wider audience? Could she handle the pressure?

She forwarded the email to Zahara with the subject line: THIS IS CRAZY?!

An hour later, Zahara burst into their dorm room, waving her phone like a victory flag. "Are you kidding me, Nia? This is HUGE!"

"It's surreal," Nia said, still staring at the email on her laptop screen. "I don't even know how they saw my photo."

Zahara flopped onto Nia's bed, grinning. "Who cares? The point is, they did. And they love it! You have to say yes."

"But what if—"

"Nope," Zahara interrupted, sitting up and pointing a finger at her. "No buts. You're doing this. You've worked so hard, and this is the payoff. You've got this, Nia."

Her confidence was contagious, but Nia couldn't shake her nerves. "It's a community exhibit, Zahara. That's... real people, not just students or professors."

"Exactly," Zahara said. "Real people who are going to see how amazing you are. Now, email them back before I do it for you."

That evening, Nia replied to Evelyn's email, thanking her for the opportunity and agreeing to meet to discuss the details. By the time she hit send, her nerves had settled into cautious excitement. She had taken the first step, and while the road ahead felt uncertain, she was ready to see where it led.

A few days later, Nia met Evelyn at The Greenlight Gallery, a modest yet elegant space tucked away in the arts district downtown. The walls were lined with pieces from local artists, each one telling its own story. Nia's heart raced as she stepped inside, trying to picture her work hanging among them.

Evelyn greeted her warmly, her presence both commanding and kind. She led Nia to a small seating area near the back of the gallery, where they discussed the exhibit.

"We're curating a series called Threads of Connection,"

Evelyn explained, her tone thoughtful. "It's about exploring the ties that bind us—to each other, to our environments, to ourselves. Your photo, Connections, embodies that beautifully. I'd love for you to expand on it and create a small series—perhaps five to seven pieces—that align with this theme."

Nia nodded, her mind already racing with ideas. "That sounds... incredible," she said, though her voice wavered slightly.

Evelyn smiled, seeming to sense her hesitation. "I know this can feel daunting, especially for a student stepping into the gallery world. But I've seen your work, Nia. You have something to say, and I'm confident you can do this."

Her words settled over Nia like a warm blanket, easing some of her nerves. "Thank you. I'll give it everything I've got."

"Good," Evelyn said, standing. "We'll provide all the logistical support you need—printing, framing, that sort of thing. The exhibit opens in six weeks, so you'll need to submit the final pieces by the end of the month. Does that timeline work for you?"

Nia nodded, her confidence growing. "It does."

When Nia returned to campus, she found Jordan waiting for her outside the dining hall. He noticed the dazed look on her face and immediately fell into step beside her. "How'd it go?"

"Good," Nia said, her voice breathy with disbelief. "Really good. She wants me to create a whole series for the exhibit—five to seven photos."

Jordan grinned. "That's amazing, Nia. I'm so proud of you."

She smiled, feeling a wave of gratitude for his steady presence in her life. "Thanks, Jordan. I'm excited, but... also terrified. That's a lot of work, and I don't even know where to start."

"You'll figure it out," he said, his tone easy but reassuring. "And I'm here if you need help. Brainstorming, carrying gear, emotional support—whatever you need, I'm in."

His words steadied her, and she nodded. "Thanks. I might take you up on that."

Back in her dorm, Zahara was already waiting, her laptop open and a list of ideas typed out. "Alright," she said, barely letting Nia put down her bag. "What's the theme? What are we working with?"

Nia laughed, sitting beside her. "Threads of Connection. Evelyn wants me to expand on the ideas in Connections—relationships, growth, all that."

Zahara's eyes lit up. "That's perfect. It's literally your wheelhouse. Let's start brainstorming moments you've captured that fit the theme. Then, we'll figure out what's missing."

For the next two hours, they worked together, combing through Nia's portfolio and jotting down potential concepts. Zahara's enthusiasm was infectious, and by the end of the night, Nia felt a spark of confidence she hadn't felt before.

As she lay in bed that night, staring at the ceiling, she thought about the journey ahead. It was daunting, yes, but it was also exhilarating. For the first time, Nia felt like she was stepping into her own story—not just documenting it, but living it.

And she was ready for whatever came next.

The list of ideas on Nia's desk had started as a source of inspiration but now felt more like a set of ticking time bombs. Each potential photo in her series came with its own set of challenges—locations to scout, shots to plan, and hours of editing she hadn't yet found in her schedule. Add to that her midterm essays, group projects, and the general demands of college life, and Nia felt like she was one misstep away from everything falling apart.

She sat in the library, her laptop open to a half-finished research paper while her camera bag sat on the floor beside her. Her mind kept drifting to the shots she needed to take for the community exhibit. The deadline for submitting her series loomed just a few weeks away, and the pressure to create something meaningful weighed on her like an anchor.

Her phone buzzed on the table.

Zahara: "Don't forget our brainstorming sesh tonight. We're gonna crush this series!"

Nia sighed, equal parts grateful for Zahara's support and overwhelmed by the constant need to keep moving. She shot back a quick reply: "Looking forward to it!"

That evening, Zahara showed up at their dorm with a stack of notebooks, a bag of snacks, and enough energy to power a small city. She spread everything out on the floor, motioning for Nia to join her.

"Alright," Zahara said, clapping her hands. "What's the vibe for this series? What do you want people to feel?"

"Connection," Nia said automatically, sitting cross-legged beside her. "I want the photos to show the relationships that shape us—the little moments that make life meaningful."

Zahara nodded, jotting down notes. "Okay, so... growth, connection, self-discovery. Those are your pillars. Now let's get specific. What are the moments in your life that speak to those ideas?"

They spent the next two hours mapping out potential shots. Zahara suggested moments Nia hadn't considered—like the quiet courtyard she'd photographed during one of her first weeks on campus or a candid picture of a classmate laughing during a late-night study session.

"You've already got so much material to work with," Zahara said, flipping through Nia's portfolio. "You just need to tie it all together."

Nia nodded, her anxiety easing slightly. Zahara's confidence in her was infectious, and for a moment, she allowed herself to believe that she could pull this off.

But the calm didn't last. The next morning, Nia's alarm went off at 6:00 a.m., and she dragged herself out of bed, groggy and irritable. She had planned an early shoot in the park to capture the soft light of dawn, but when she arrived, her camera battery died after just a few shots.

Back at her dorm, she realized she'd forgotten to charge it the night before, too distracted by an essay she had rushed to complete before the deadline. Frustrated, she slammed her camera onto her desk and sank into her chair, rubbing her temples.

By the time she met Jordan for lunch, her mood was sour. He greeted her with a cheerful smile, but Nia barely looked up from her phone as she picked at her sandwich.

"You okay?" Jordan asked, his brow furrowing.

"Fine," she mumbled.

"You sure? You seem stressed."

"I said I'm fine," she snapped, louder than she intended.

Jordan blinked, taken aback. "Okay... I'll leave it alone."

Guilt twisted in her stomach, but she couldn't bring herself to apologize. The truth was, she wasn't fine—not even close.

The next few days were a blur of missed sleep and mounting pressure. Nia barely kept up with her assignments, skipped meals, and avoided her friends to focus on editing photos and planning shoots. But no matter how hard she worked, it felt like she was barely keeping her head above water.

Everything came to a head one night when Zahara returned to their dorm to find Nia staring at her laptop, tears welling in her eyes.

"What happened?" Zahara asked, setting her bag down and kneeling beside her.

"I missed the deadline for my psych paper," Nia said, her voice shaking. "I was so focused on the exhibit that I completely forgot about it. And my photos—none of them are turning out the way I want. I feel like I'm failing at everything."

Zahara frowned, reaching for Nia's hand. "Nia, you're not failing. You're just trying to do too much at once."

"I can't ask for help," Nia said, her voice cracking. "I have to prove I can handle this on my own."

"That's ridiculous," Zahara said, squeezing her hand. "Asking for help doesn't mean you're weak. It means you're human. And you've got people who care about you—me, Jordan, your family. Let us help you."

Nia wiped her eyes, Zahara's words sinking in. She thought about the way she had snapped at Jordan, the times she had pushed Zahara away when she tried to offer support. She didn't want to keep shutting people out.

"You're right," she said softly. "I can't do this alone."

The next morning, Nia made a conscious effort to ask for help. She reached out to her psych professor to explain the missed assignment and was surprised by how understanding they were.

She texted Jordan to apologize for her outburst, and he replied immediately: *No worries. Let me know how I can help.*

When she told Zahara about her plan to delegate tasks and set a more manageable schedule, her roommate grinned. "Now you're talking. Let's figure this out."

Together, they created a plan that balanced her academic work with her photography commitments. Zahara even volunteered to scout locations and hold reflectors during Nia's shoots, while Jordan offered to review her photos and provide feedback.

The shift in Nia's mindset was slow but steady. She learned to pace herself, tackling one task at a time instead of trying to do everything at once. With Zahara's help, she finalized the themes for her series: Growth through connection, finding strength in vulnerability, and Discovering beauty in the mundane.

One evening, as she reviewed her latest batch of photos, Nia felt a sense of calm she hadn't experienced in weeks. She wasn't just surviving—she was learning. And for the first time, she believed she could pull this off.

By the time the exhibit deadline approached, Nia had found a rhythm that worked. She still felt the weight of her responsibilities, but she no longer carried it alone.

In learning to lean on her friends, she realized that strength wasn't about doing everything on her own—it was about knowing when to ask for help and trusting others to be there when she needed them.

Nia hadn't planned on making Jordan such a regular part of her photography process, but somehow, he had become her default partner. He carried tripods, adjusted lighting when she needed an extra set of hands, and always seemed to know when she needed a break. Their dynamic was easy, a quiet rhythm that made the weight of her responsibilities feel a little lighter.

"You're surprisingly good at this whole assistant thing," Nia teased one afternoon as they set up for a shoot in the campus greenhouse.

Jordan grinned, adjusting the reflector to bounce light onto the cascading vines she was photographing. "What can I say? I have a talent for standing around and holding things."

They both laughed, the sound echoing in the quiet space. These moments of levity were what Nia had come to treasure most. With Jordan, she didn't feel the need to impress anyone or prove herself. He had a way of grounding her, reminding her to enjoy the process instead of obsessing over the end result.

One particularly tough shoot tested her patience. Nia had envisioned capturing the perfect interplay of shadows and sunlight on the stone arches behind the library. But the light wasn't cooperating, her camera settings felt wrong, and every shot seemed lifeless.

She sighed heavily, lowering her camera. "This isn't working. None of it feels right."

Jordan, sitting nearby with his notebook—something he had recently started carrying again—looked up. "What's wrong with it?"

"Everything," she said, her frustration bubbling over. "The angles, the lighting, the composition—it's all wrong. I don't even know why I'm doing this anymore. What if I'm not good enough for the exhibit? What if Evelyn made a mistake picking me?"

Jordan stood and walked over, gently taking the camera from her hands. "You're spiraling," he said softly. "Take a breath."

Nia looked at him, the sting of tears threatening to blur her vision. "I don't know if I can do this, Jordan. What if I fail?"

"You won't," he said firmly. "You've already done so much, Nia. Remember the showcase? You blew people away. And you're just getting started. Do you know how many people wish they could put themselves out there the way you do?"

She blinked, his words cutting through the storm of doubt in her mind. "You really think that?"

"I know that," he said, his voice steady. "You have something to say, and people want to hear it. Don't let one bad shoot make you forget that."

His encouragement stayed with her as they packed up and headed back to campus. The sun had set, leaving the sky painted with streaks of deep indigo and orange. They walked in comfortable silence for a while, the weight of the day slowly lifting from Nia's shoulders.

"Thanks for today," she said finally, glancing at him.

Jordan smiled. "Anytime. Besides, I like hanging out with you. Even if it means lugging around all your stuff."

She laughed, nudging him playfully. "Careful, or I might start calling you my full-time assistant."

"Deal," he said, his grin widening. "As long as you pay me in snacks."

The easy banter made her chest feel warm, but there was something deeper stirring beneath the surface—something she hadn't fully acknowledged until now. As they reached the steps of the dorm, Nia paused, looking up at the stars that dotted the night sky.

"What's on your mind?" Jordan asked, his voice gentle.

She hesitated, the words tangled in her throat. How could she explain what she was feeling without ruining the delicate balance they had?

"Nothing," she said instead, forcing a smile. "Just tired."

But as she watched him walk away, she couldn't shake the realization that had settled quietly in her heart: she was falling for him.

Over the next few days, the thought stayed with her, both thrilling and terrifying. She found herself noticing the little things about Jordan—the way his brow furrowed when he concentrated, the way he listened so intently when she spoke, as if every word mattered.

Their friendship continued to grow, each interaction layered with unspoken understanding. Jordan had started bringing his sketchpad to her shoots more often, rediscovering his own creative spark as he helped her with hers.

"I forgot how much I loved writing," he admitted one afternoon as they sat on a bench near the campus fountain.

Nia looked at him, surprised. "You used to write?"

He nodded, pulling out a small notebook he had been scribbling in. "I stopped after high school. Life got busy, and I guess I just didn't make time for it anymore."

"Well, you're really good," she said after skimming a few lines he had written. "You should keep at it."

He smiled, a little sheepish. "Maybe I will."

One evening, as they reviewed her latest batch of photos, Jordan pointed to an image of the greenhouse. "This one's amazing," he said. "It feels like you're looking through someone's eyes, like you're part of the moment."

Nia stared at the photo, then at him. "You always know exactly what to say," she said softly.

"That's because I believe in you," he said, meeting her gaze.

The weight of his words settled over her, and for a moment, everything else faded away—the pressure of the exhibit, the chaos of her schedule, the noise of her own self-doubt.

"Thank you," she said, her voice almost a whisper.

"For what?"

"For being here," she said simply.

Later that night, as Nia lay in bed, staring at the ceiling, she let herself fully accept what she had been feeling. She cared about Jordan—not just as a friend, but as someone who had become an integral part of her life.

It scared her to think about what might happen if she told him, but it scared her even more to think about losing the connection they had built. For now, she decided, it was enough to let the feeling exist, to carry it quietly as she focused on the work ahead.

But deep down, she knew that this was a moment of growth, a step toward something new. And no matter what came next, she was grateful to have him by her side.

The hum of the studio was constant—a faint buzz of lights, the soft whir of her laptop fan, and the click of Nia's mouse as she edited her latest batch of photos. She'd been spending nearly every evening there, the hours slipping by as she tinkered with lighting and contrast, cropping and reframing until each image felt just right. Her focus was razor-sharp, but it came at a cost she hadn't fully realized.

Back at the dorm, Zahara barely saw her anymore. Their once-regular late-night chats had dwindled to passing comments and brief nods as Nia rushed out the door. The empty takeout containers on Nia's desk were a testament to how little time she spent in their shared space.

One evening, Zahara decided to wait up for her. It was well past midnight when the door finally creaked open, and Nia walked in, her bag slung over her shoulder and exhaustion etched into her face. She barely looked at Zahara as she tossed her things onto her desk.

"Hey," Zahara said, sitting up on her bed.

"Hey," Nia replied distractedly, her focus already on her laptop.

"You've been out late a lot," Zahara said, trying to keep her tone light.

"Yeah, I've just been busy," Nia mumbled, not looking up.

Zahara's patience snapped. "Busy with what? Avoiding me?"

Nia froze, turning to face her. "What? No. I'm just working on my exhibit."

"I get that," Zahara said, her voice tight. "But it's like I don't even exist anymore. You come home late, you barely talk to me, and we haven't hung out in weeks. I've been here for you through everything, Nia, but it feels like you've completely forgotten about me."

Nia blinked, caught off guard by the frustration in Zahara's tone. "Zahara, it's not like that. I'm just under so much pressure right now—this exhibit is everything to me."

"And what about me?" Zahara asked, her voice rising. "Do I not matter? Do our late-night talks and all the times I've supported you not count for anything?"

"That's not fair," Nia said defensively. "You know how much this exhibit means to me."

"And you know how much our friendship means to me," Zahara shot back. "But it doesn't feel like it matters to you anymore."

The words hit Nia like a punch to the gut. She opened her mouth to respond but found herself at a loss. Zahara's expression was a mix of hurt and anger, and it made Nia realize how much she had been taking her friend for granted.

"I'm sorry," Nia said finally, her voice barely above a whisper. "I didn't mean to make you feel like this."

"Intentions don't matter, Nia. Actions do," Zahara said, standing. "I've been trying to be patient, but I can't keep pretending this doesn't hurt. Friendship isn't something you can put on hold when it's inconvenient."

Zahara grabbed her phone and left the room, leaving Nia alone with her thoughts. The door clicked shut behind her, and the silence that followed was deafening.

The confrontation played on a loop in Nia's mind for the rest of the night. She sat at her desk, staring blankly at her laptop screen, the images in front of her blurring together. Zahara's words echoed in her head, each one cutting deeper than the last.

Had she really been that selfish?

She thought back to all the moments she had brushed Zahara off or promised to spend time together "later," only to disappear into her work. At the time, it had felt justified—after all, wasn't she working toward something important? But now, she saw how one-sided that reasoning had been.

Her stomach twisted with guilt.

The next day, Nia found Zahara in their favorite spot at the campus café, headphones in and a textbook spread out in front of her. Nia hesitated for a moment, then approached cautiously.

"Hey," she said softly.

Zahara glanced up, her expression unreadable. "Hey."

"Can I sit?"

Zahara shrugged.

Nia sat down, wringing her hands nervously. "I'm really sorry about last night," she began. "I didn't realize how much I've been shutting you out, but that's not an excuse. You were right—I've been so focused on my own stuff that I stopped being a good friend. And that's not okay."

Zahara's shoulders softened slightly, though she still looked guarded. "It just felt like I didn't matter to you anymore," she said quietly. "Like I was just... there."

"You do matter," Nia said earnestly. "You've been my rock

since the day we met, and I've been awful at showing you how much I appreciate that. I'm so sorry, Zahara. I don't want to lose our friendship."

There was a long pause, and Nia held her breath, waiting for Zahara's response.

Finally, Zahara sighed, closing her textbook. "I forgive you," she said, her voice softer now. "But we need to work on this, okay? Friendship is a two-way street. I'll always have your back, but you have to let me in."

Nia nodded, relief washing over her. "I will. I promise."

Zahara smiled faintly. "Good. Now, let's get coffee before my next class. My treat."

The tension between them eased after that, but the confrontation left a lasting impression on Nia. She realized that her relationships were just as important as her work, if not more so. Balancing the two wouldn't be easy, but she was determined to do better.

That evening, she set aside time to hang out with Zahara. They ordered pizza, played music, and talked about everything except the exhibit. It felt like old times, and for the first time in weeks, Nia felt lighter.

As they laughed over a silly memory, Nia silently vowed to never take her friendships for granted again.

Zahara caught her looking thoughtful and nudged her playfully. "What's that face for?"

"Just thinking about how lucky I am," Nia said with a smile.

"Damn right you are," Zahara said with a grin.

Their bond, though tested, felt stronger than ever. And as Nia lay in bed that night, she felt a renewed sense of clarity. The exhibit was important, but so were the people who had been there for her every step of the way.

From that moment on, Nia resolved to find a balance—to give her work the attention it deserved without sacrificing the relationships that gave her life meaning.

Chapter 10
Crossroads and Connections

The Greenlight Gallery stood on a quiet street corner, its tall windows glowing warmly against the twilight. As Nia approached, her camera bag slung over her shoulder, she felt a mixture of excitement and anxiety bubbling in her chest. Tonight was the night she'd been working toward—a culmination of late nights, creative breakthroughs, and moments of doubt. Her photos, so deeply personal, were now on display for the world to see.

Inside, the gallery was already a hive of activity. Staff moved briskly, adjusting lighting and finalizing details. The air carried a faint hum of conversation mixed with the scent of fresh flowers that adorned a table near the entrance. Nia's breath hitched as she spotted her collection hanging on a wall near the center of the room.

She approached the display slowly, taking in the sight of her photos framed and illuminated by carefully placed lights. Each one told a story: Zahara laughing under the tree, Jordan's quiet contemplation by the fountain, the golden light spilling across the courtyard that had once been her private retreat. Seeing them together like this filled her with a strange sense of validation—her journey, captured in snapshots, now felt real.

"You're here early," came a familiar voice. Nia turned to see Evelyn, the gallery curator, walking over with a clipboard in hand.

"I wanted to take it all in before it got crowded," Nia admitted, smiling nervously.

Evelyn glanced at the display and nodded approvingly. "Your work is incredible, Nia. The emotional depth, the way you capture connection—it's going to resonate with a lot of people tonight."

"Thank you," Nia said, the words barely above a whisper.

Not long after, her parents arrived, their familiar presence both grounding and heartwarming. Her mom's eyes widened as she took in the display. "Oh, Nia, these are beautiful!" she said, pulling her daughter into a tight hug.

Nia blushed. "Thanks, Mom."

Her dad stepped closer to the photos, adjusting his glasses as he examined them. "This one," he said, pointing to the shot of the courtyard, "it feels... peaceful. Like you can hear the quiet just by looking at it."

Nia's chest tightened with emotion. Her dad wasn't one for many words, but when he did speak, it always carried weight.

Her mom, ever the documentarian, insisted on taking several photos of Nia in front of her work. "Smile! No, bigger! This is your moment!" she said, her enthusiasm contagious.

As Nia posed, she felt a flicker of pride. Having her parents here, seeing their joy and support, made all the hard work worth it.

The gallery began to fill quickly as the evening progressed. Zahara was next to arrive, bursting through the doors in a swirl of energy. She spotted Nia immediately and beelined for her, dragging a reluctant Jordan behind her.

"There's the star of the night!" Zahara exclaimed, throwing her arms around Nia. "Look at this setup! Front and center, as it should be."

Nia laughed, Zahara's excitement helping to ease her nerves. "You think it's okay?"

"Okay? Girl, it's amazing," Zahara said, stepping back to study the display. "I told you your work was gallery-worthy. But do you ever listen to me? No."

Jordan chuckled, standing quietly beside them. He didn't say much at first, but the way he looked at Nia—proud and steady—said more than words could.

"You did good," he finally said, his voice soft.

"Thanks," Nia replied, her cheeks warming.

As more people arrived, Nia was surprised to see several familiar faces from campus—her project group members, classmates, and even some of her professors. Leila, the most blunt of her group partners, greeted her with an enthusiastic handshake.

"Wow, Nia," Leila said, gesturing toward the photos. "These are... way better than I expected. No offense."

"Uh, thanks?" Nia replied, laughing.

Chris, who had contributed the least to their project but somehow always showed up for social events, chimed in. "Seriously, though, this is impressive. Congrats."

The room buzzed with energy as guests moved from display to display, sipping on drinks and murmuring appreciatively. Nia found herself in a constant stream of introductions and conversations, explaining the inspiration behind her work to strangers who genuinely seemed to connect with it.

At one point, a woman paused in front of the photo of Zahara and turned to Nia. "This one—it feels so alive. Like I can hear her laugh," she said, smiling warmly.

"That's my best friend," Nia said, her voice tinged with pride. "She's pretty amazing."

Across the room, Zahara was playfully posing for another photo with one of Nia's project partners, clearly soaking up the attention.

"Of course she is," the woman said. "But you captured something deeper. It's rare to see that kind of connection in a photo."

Nia thanked her, the comment sinking in. Moments like these made the nerves and sleepless nights feel worthwhile.

As the evening wore on, Nia felt an unexpected wave of calm wash over her. Everywhere she looked, there were people she cared about—her parents, Zahara, Jordan, her classmates—and even people she didn't know, all coming together because of her work.

She watched as her dad spoke quietly with another guest, likely offering his own interpretation of the photos. Her mom was chatting animatedly with Zahara, probably telling embarrassing childhood stories. Jordan stood nearby, leaning casually against the wall but keeping her within his line of sight, ready to step in if she needed anything.

The unity of the moment was overwhelming in the best way. Nia realized that her photos had done more than tell her story— they had created connections between people, sparked conversations, and brought her closer to the people who mattered most.

By the time the gallery began to empty, Nia's nerves had transformed into a deep sense of gratitude. Standing in the middle of the room, surrounded by her work and the love of her community, she felt a flicker of something she hadn't experienced in a long time: belonging.

This was her moment, not just as an artist, but as a person who had grown, stumbled, and found her way back to the things that mattered. And for the first time, she allowed herself to fully embrace it.

The cool night air hit Nia's face as she stepped outside the gallery, letting the door close softly behind her. Inside, the hum of conversation and clinking glasses continued, but she needed a moment away from the crowd to breathe. The night sky was clear, the stars scattered like faint pinpricks against the dark canvas above. She wrapped her arms around herself, both to ward off the chill and to steady the emotions swirling inside her.

She was proud—overwhelmingly so—but also exhausted. The exhibit was everything she had hoped for, but the weight of the evening, of baring her soul through her photos, left her feeling vulnerable in a way she hadn't expected.

The sound of the door creaking open startled her, and she turned to see Jordan stepping out, his hands tucked into his jacket pockets. He offered her a small smile, one that was both warm and tentative.

"Thought you might be out here," he said, closing the door behind him.

Nia returned his smile, a little sheepish. "Needed a breather."

"Big night," he said, leaning against the brick wall beside her. "I don't blame you."

They stood in silence for a moment, the quiet punctuated only by the faint sounds of the city in the distance. Nia glanced at Jordan, his profile softened by the glow of a nearby streetlamp. He seemed calm, but there was a thoughtful intensity in his eyes, as if he was working up the courage to say something.

"You know," he began, his voice low, "watching you tonight... it made me think about everything we've been through this semester."

Nia tilted her head, her chest tightening slightly. "What do you mean?"

Jordan shifted, his gaze dropping to the ground for a moment before meeting hers. "I mean us. You and me. It hasn't exactly been easy, has it?"

"No," she admitted, her voice soft. "It hasn't."

"I've been thinking about the times I let you down," he said, his tone steady but laced with regret. "The way I took you for granted, how I made you feel like you were carrying the weight of everything alone. I hate that I did that to you."

Nia's breath caught. She had spent so much time trying to move past the hurt, to focus on her work and her friendships, that hearing him acknowledge it so openly brought the emotions rushing back. But there was something different now—something healing in his words.

"You weren't the only one," she said after a moment, her voice trembling slightly. "I pushed you away too. I didn't know how to let you in when I felt like I was drowning."

Jordan nodded, his expression thoughtful. "I think we both

made mistakes. But... I also think we've learned a lot. At least, I have."

She looked at him, searching his face for sincerity. "What have you learned?"

"That you're one of the most incredible people I've ever met," he said simply. "And that I don't want to lose you."

The honesty in his voice left her speechless. She had always cared about Jordan—deeply—but she had buried those feelings under layers of hurt and self-protection. Hearing him say those words, seeing the vulnerability in his eyes, cracked something open inside her.

"I care about you too," she said finally, her voice barely above a whisper. "But relationships aren't easy. They take work, and... I'm scared of messing it up again."

"We'll probably mess up," Jordan said with a small smile. "But I think we're worth the effort. Don't you?"

Nia felt her heart swell, a mixture of hope and fear colliding. She thought about the moments they had shared recently—the quiet walks, the laughter, the way he had shown up for her when she needed him most. He had become more than a friend, more than a source of comfort. He was someone who saw her, who believed in her, even when she struggled to believe in herself.

"I think we are," she said softly, her eyes meeting his.

Jordan's smile widened, and he took a small step closer. "So... we give it a shot? You and me?"

Nia nodded, her heart pounding. "Yeah. Let's try."

For a moment, neither of them moved, the weight of the decision settling between them. Then, slowly, Jordan leaned in, his gaze never leaving hers. Nia felt herself move toward him, their faces inches apart, the world around them fading into the background.

When their lips met, it was soft and tentative, a gentle exploration that spoke of trust and new beginnings. The kiss wasn't rushed or dramatic—it was simply theirs, a quiet moment that felt both fragile and unshakable.

When they pulled apart, Jordan rested his forehead against hers, his breath warm against her skin. "That felt right," he said, his voice barely audible.

"It did," Nia replied, her lips curving into a small smile.

They stood like that for a moment longer before the sound of the gallery door opening behind them broke the spell. Nia stepped back slightly, her cheeks flushing as a few guests spilled out onto the sidewalk, chatting animatedly.

"We should probably head back inside," she said, glancing at Jordan.

"Yeah," he said, his smile returning. "But just so you know, I'm not letting you disappear on me in there."

Nia laughed, the sound light and genuine. "Deal."

As they walked back into the gallery together, their shoulders brushing, Nia felt a sense of peace she hadn't experienced in a long time. The exhibit, the photos, the people—all of it mattered. But this moment, this connection, was something she knew she wanted to hold onto.

For the first time, the future didn't feel so uncertain. It felt like the beginning of something beautiful.

As the gallery began to quiet down, with many guests leaving and the hum of conversations softening, Nia noticed Zahara standing alone near one of her photos. It was the shot that had always meant the most to her: Zahara laughing under the oak tree, with Jordan in the background, holding a leaf to the light. The photo captured so much of what she had experienced that semester—connection, growth, and the joy of small, fleeting moments.

Zahara studied the image intently, her arms crossed, her expression unreadable. Nia hesitated, unsure how to approach. Despite their earlier reconciliation, she knew there were still things left unsaid. Taking a deep breath, she walked over, her footsteps light on the polished floor.

"You know," Zahara said without turning, "I still think my laugh is the star of this picture. You should've titled it 'Radiance.'"

Nia laughed softly, the tension in her chest easing a little. "I thought about it. But 'Roots' felt more fitting."

Zahara finally turned to face her, a small smile tugging at the corners of her mouth. "Roots, huh? That's deep. I'll give you that."

They stood in silence for a moment, the photo between them. Nia shuffled nervously before speaking. "Zahara, I just... I want to thank you. For everything. For pushing me, supporting me, and for sticking around, even when I've been the worst friend ever."

Zahara raised an eyebrow, leaning casually against the wall. "The worst friend ever? That's dramatic, even for you."

"I'm serious," Nia said, her voice quiet but earnest. "I got so wrapped up in my own world that I forgot to show up for you. And that's not okay. You've always been there for me, and I didn't return the favor. I'm sorry."

Zahara's expression softened, and she let out a small sigh. "I won't lie, Nia. It hurt. You disappearing like that, not answering texts, brushing me off—it sucked. But I also know how much this exhibit meant to you. And I know you weren't doing it to be malicious. You just... lost sight of things."

Nia nodded, guilt pressing against her chest. "I did. And I hate that I let it happen."

"Look," Zahara said, placing a hand on Nia's shoulder, "we're all allowed to get a little lost sometimes. But friendships, real friendships, require balance. You can't just check out when life gets chaotic. That's when you need your people the most."

"I get that now," Nia said. "And I promise, I'll do better. I'll make time, even when things get crazy. You're too important to me to let this happen again."

Zahara studied her for a moment before breaking into a grin. "Okay, fine. Apology accepted. But if you ever pull that disappearing act again, I'm stealing your camera and taking selfies on it until your memory card's full."

Nia laughed, relief flooding through her. "Deal."

Their conversation shifted to lighter topics as they moved through the gallery together. Zahara teased Nia mercilessly about her newfound relationship with Jordan.

"So," Zahara said, nudging Nia with her elbow, "are you going to start taking moody black-and-white portraits of him now? You know, the tortured artist boyfriend aesthetic?"

"Stop," Nia groaned, covering her face. "We're just figuring things out."

Zahara smirked. "Sure, sure. But for the record, I approve. He's a good guy, and he obviously adores you. Just don't let him monopolize all your creative energy."

"Noted," Nia said, rolling her eyes but smiling.

They paused in front of another photo, this one of the quiet courtyard bathed in golden light. Zahara tilted her head, studying it. "You've got something special, Nia. Your photos—they're more than just pretty pictures. They make people feel something. That's rare."

"Thanks," Nia said, her cheeks flushing.

"And don't think I'm saying this just because I'm in one of them," Zahara added with a wink.

They laughed together, the tension from earlier now completely gone.

By the end of the night, the gallery was nearly empty, and Nia felt a calm sense of satisfaction settle over her. Zahara helped her pack up a few things, the two of them working in comfortable silence.

As they walked outside, the cool air brushing against their faces, Zahara looked at Nia with a mischievous grin. "So, what's next for the great Nia? Another exhibit? A world tour? A coffee table book?"

Nia laughed. "Let's get through tonight first. But honestly, I'm just excited to keep creating. And to actually spend time with my friends again."

"Good answer," Zahara said, throwing an arm around Nia's shoulders. "Because we're getting pizza after this. No excuses."

Nia smiled, her heart full. The exhibit was a success, but this moment—with Zahara's arm around her and the promise of greasy, late-night pizza—felt like the real victory.

As they walked toward their favorite spot, Nia realized how lucky she was to have Zahara in her life. Their friendship wasn't perfect, but it was strong, built on trust, honesty, and a shared understanding that neither of them had to face life's chaos alone.

And as far as Nia was concerned, that was more than enough.

As the last of the guests filtered out of The Greenlight Gallery, the hum of conversation gave way to a profound stillness. Nia stood near the entrance, watching as the gallery staff began tidying up. Zahara and Jordan had left a few moments earlier, promising to meet her for a late-night pizza celebration. Her parents had also gone home, her mom practically glowing with pride and her dad offering a quiet, heartfelt "You've done good, kid" before they left.

Now, with the gallery nearly empty, Nia found herself alone amidst her photos, the quiet amplifying the weight of the moment. She wandered toward her display, each photo a window into her journey over the past semester.

The shot of Zahara laughing under the tree caught her eye first. The sunlight streaming through the branches, the carefree tilt of Zahara's head—it perfectly captured the energy and warmth that Zahara had brought into her life. Nia smiled, her chest tightening with gratitude.

Next, her gaze fell on the photo of Jordan at the fountain, the golden hour light accentuating his thoughtful expression. That photo had been a turning point for her, a moment when she realized how much he meant to her and how photography had helped her see him—and herself—more clearly.

She moved to the image of the quiet courtyard, a place that had been her refuge during the chaotic first weeks of the semester. The golden light, the long shadows—it wasn't just a photo of a place; it was a photo of a feeling, of finding calm amidst uncertainty.

As she studied each piece, Nia felt a wave of emotions—pride, relief, and a deep sense of gratitude. She had started this journey feeling lost, unsure of her place in the world, and now she stood here, not just as an artist, but as someone who had grown stronger through every challenge.

Nia found herself drawn to a bench in the corner of the gallery, tucked away but with a clear view of her display. She sat down, pulling her journal from her bag. She hadn't written in weeks, the busyness of preparing for the exhibit consuming her days. But now, in the quiet aftermath, the urge to put her thoughts into words felt undeniable.

She flipped to a blank page, her pen hovering for a moment before she began to write:

This semester has been a whirlwind. When I first stepped onto campus, I felt like a blank canvas—empty, unsure of what picture I wanted to create. I was overwhelmed, scared, and constantly questioning if I was enough.

She paused, glancing up at her photos.

Photography became my way of finding answers. It forced me to stop, to look, to really see. Through the lens, I began to notice things I had overlooked before—the way light filters through leaves, the quiet strength in someone's expression, the beauty in fleeting moments. Photography gave me a voice when I couldn't find the words.

Her pen moved steadily now, the words flowing as if they had been waiting for this moment.

But this journey hasn't just been about art. It's been about balance—learning to navigate the pull between ambition and relationships, between growth and reflection. There were times I got it wrong. I let my focus narrow too much, and I hurt the people who mattered most. But they stayed. They reminded me that life isn't meant to be lived alone. It's about connection, about showing up for the people who show up for you.

She thought of Zahara's unwavering support, even when Nia had neglected their friendship. She thought of Jordan's quiet patience and his ability to ground her when self-doubt crept in. She thought of her parents, who had always believed in her, even when she hadn't believed in herself.

Resilience, I've learned, isn't just about pushing through. It's about knowing when to lean on others, when to ask for help, and when to pause. It's about finding the courage to be vulnerable, to open yourself up to the people and the moments that make life meaningful.

Her pen slowed as she reached the end of the page. She added one final line:

To everyone who has been part of this journey—thank you. You've taught me that the most beautiful things in life are the connections we create and the effort we put into them.

Nia closed the journal, running her fingers over the cover as she leaned back on the bench. A sense of peace settled over her. The exhibit, the photos, the journey—it wasn't about perfection. It was about progress, about learning and growing and becoming.

She looked at the photos one last time, her heart full. This was her story, captured in fragments of light and shadow, in moments of joy and struggle. And it wasn't just her story—it was theirs, too. The people who had shaped her, supported her, challenged her.

As she stood to leave, she pulled her camera from her bag. Walking to the center of the room, she set it on a tripod, adjusting the angle to capture the entire gallery. She pressed the timer and stepped into the frame, standing amidst her photos.

The camera clicked, freezing the moment in time.

It wasn't just a photo of the gallery. It was a photo of who she had become—a person who had learned to balance ambition with relationships, to find beauty in the everyday, and to build connections that made her stronger.

And as she turned off the camera and slung it over her shoulder, she knew this was just the beginning of her story. here.

ACKNOWLEDGMENTS

Writing a book is a journey, and like any meaningful journey, it is never taken alone. While this book bears my name, it is the result of countless hands, minds, and hearts that have shaped and supported it along the way.

First and foremost, I want to express my deepest gratitude to *The Inkwell Publishing Company*. To say this book would not exist without your belief in it is an understatement. From the moment you embraced my vision for *Crossroads and Connections*, you treated it with care, respect, and an unparalleled passion that made me feel seen as an author and as a storyteller. Your team—every single one of you—poured your energy into shaping this work into its best possible form, and I am forever indebted to you for your expertise and unwavering commitment. Thank you for giving my words a home and for championing this story from the very beginning.

I owe a very special thanks to my editor, Demetri Long—my best friend, collaborator, and guiding light throughout this entire process. Demetri, I don't even know where to begin. You have been my rock, my confidant, and my fiercest advocate from day one. Thank you for pushing me to dig deeper when I wanted to stop, for reminding me of the story's heart when I felt lost, and for always knowing exactly what this book needed even when I doubted myself. Your edits were not just corrections; they were revelations. You saw potential in every draft, in every chapter, and most importantly, in me. This book would not be what it is without your talent, your insight, and your friendship. Thank you for being my partner in this labor of love, and for making me laugh through the hardest parts. I hope this acknowledgment can capture even a fraction of the gratitude I have for you.

To my friends, who have walked beside me through every stage of this process: you are the chosen family that has held me together through the long nights, the self-doubt, and the inevitable caffeine-fueled meltdowns. Thank you for listening to me ramble endlessly about characters and plots, for showing up to every celebration and every crisis, and for believing in me even when I didn't. You have been my light in the darkest of times, and your encouragement means more to me than I could ever put into words.

To the readers of *Crossroads and Connections*, thank you for opening this book, for giving it your time, your attention, and your heart. I hope that Nia's journey resonates with you and reminds you of the beauty in small moments, the strength in connection, and the courage it takes to embrace change. Your willingness to walk alongside these characters, to see the world through their eyes, is a gift I will never take for granted. This book was written for you, and I hope it leaves a mark on your heart as it has on mine.

To the countless people whose stories have shaped this book in ways seen and unseen, thank you for inspiring me. Whether we crossed paths briefly or shared long conversations, your resilience, strength, and humanity have deeply influenced the pages of this story. You are the heartbeat of this book, and I am endlessly grateful for the ways you've enriched my perspective and my life.

Finally, I want to acknowledge the quiet moments, the small victories, and the spaces where creativity blooms. Thank you to the late nights spent scribbling in notebooks, to the coffee shops that fueled my ideas, and to the walks that cleared my mind. Thank you to the setbacks that taught me patience and the breakthroughs that reminded me why I write. This book is a testament to the power of persistence, passion, and connection, and I am so proud to share it with the world.

To every person, every moment, and every inspiration that has brought *Crossroads and Connections* to life: thank you. You are part of this story, and I carry your influence with me always.

ABOUT THE AUTHOR

La'Shayla Godfrey is a young, emerging author from Cincinnati, known for her passion for storytelling and her unique perspective. With a natural talent for capturing emotions and experiences, La'Shayla's writing reflects both her creativity and her deep connection to her roots. As a new voice in the literary world, she aims to inspire and connect with readers through powerful narratives that resonate with a wide range of audiences.

ABOUT THE PUBLISHER

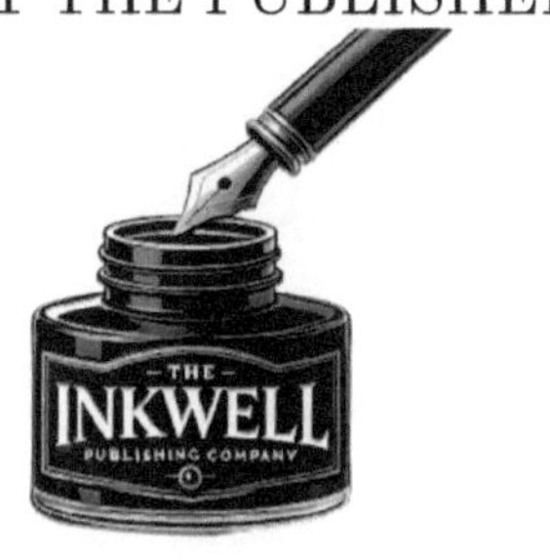

The Inkwell Publishing Company is a forward-thinking literary hub dedicated to reshaping the publishing landscape. The company is driven by the belief that ideas have the power to inspire change, spark creativity, and connect humanity. At The Inkwell, authors are empowered to share their unique voices, and readers are invited into a community that values thought-provoking stories and meaningful engagement.
More than just a publisher, The Inkwell Publishing Company is a platform for innovation and collaboration. It champions new ways of thinking about literature and publishing, challenging traditional norms to create an inclusive, transformative space for creators and audiences alike. Through its commitment to quality, originality, and authenticity, The Inkwell is shaping the future of storytelling—one idea at a time.